Playing u

In addition to being a writer for children, Alan primary school. He is als speaker in schools and at book events. He lives in Liverpool with his wife and four children.

Alan Gibbons won the Blue Peter Book Award in the 'Book I Couldn't Put Down' category for *Shadow of the Minotaur*, which was also short-listed for the Carnegie Medal.

Other books by the same author

Playing with Fire

Alan Gibbons

A Dolphin
Paperback

First published in Great Britain in 1996
by Orion Children's Books
First published in paperback 1997
by Dolphin paperbacks
Reissued 2003 by Dolphin paperbacks
a division of the Orion Publishing Group Ltd
Orion House
5 Upper St Martin's Lane
London WC2H 9EA

A catalogue record for this book is available
from the British Library.

Printed in Great Britain by
Clays Ltd, St Ives plc

ISBN 1 85881 385 9

One

*H*E COULD HAVE GONE ANYWHERE. AUNT CAROL could have sent him to any of a dozen schools. Liverpool was a big enough city, the sort of place you could get lost in. But that wasn't Kevin McGovern's style at all. Quietly starting a new life would be far too easy. He was trouble, always had been, always would be. As Cheryl kicked her way through the piles of sodden, windblown leaves that choked the pavement that October morning, she was a battlefield of conflicting emotions. There were moments when, despite everything that had happened, she found herself actually looking forward to the day ahead, anticipating her cousin's arrival. He was everything she wasn't: sharp, fierce, competitive, a spit in the world's eye. He had more bottle than Schweppes. Then she would remember. She almost gagged on the memories that came flooding back.

'I hate you, Kev,' she announced bitterly to the swirling wind. It was the strangest day. Heavy, blustery showers followed by blazing sunlight. As changeable as … well, life, since Kevin got himself into bother. One day in July he had cracked the whole world wide open. And Cheryl was no fan of the unexpected. She couldn't even read a book without leafing through to the final chapter to check out the ending. What Cheryl liked was routine, and she knew for certain that Kevin's arrival would shatter it into fragments. She found herself twisting her hair until it hurt. She always did that when she was nervous. Even when she was little she used to curl up, winding her hair round her finger. Mum had even had to put a glove on her hand at bedtime to stop her making a bald patch.

'Why here?' she groaned, still tugging at the frizzy lock. 'Why here?'

But there was no wishing him away. He was coming. To Cropper Lane, *her* Cropper Lane, and he was bringing his guilty secret with him. Cheryl knew the secret, of course. There was no hiding something as serious as a man's death. She just thanked her lucky stars that it had all happened in a different part of town. It wasn't common knowledge in her neighbourhood – at least not yet. As she trudged into school she could feel Kevin's secret like a dead weight inside her.

'Cheryl!'

Oh great, there was the dead weight, right on cue. She half-turned to greet him. Kevin was a striking boy, not overly tall but lean and spare. His olive-skinned face seemed almost fleshless. The hollow cheeks and hooked nose might have made him ugly but for his oval brown eyes that everybody seemed to comment on.

'Hi there, Kevin.' Her voice was flat, her anxiety too much to disguise.

'What's the matter with you?'

'Headache.'

Heartache might have been more like it, but what she really meant was pain in the neck.

'Lighten up, Cheryl,' said Kevin. 'You look like somebody who's lost a fiver and found a quid.'

'Oh, leave me alone, Kev. I can't act as if nothing happened. It's only a few weeks, you know.'

Kevin's eyes dulled. 'Not you too. Why won't anybody let it drop? The social worker was round on Friday.'

'Mrs Williams?'

'No, Willy's on holiday. Some speccy four-eyes who looked at me like I belonged in a zoo.'

'I bet she never.'

'She did. She couldn't wait to get back in her car. None of them care about me.'

'Mrs Williams seems very nice.'

'Huh, Willy's just another do-gooder.'

'So what did she have to say, the social worker?'

'Same old guff Willy comes out with. I just clammed up on her. She hated that.'

Cheryl rolled her eyes. 'No wonder.'

'Well, they think they're God's gift. What makes them think they can tell me what to do?'

'Somebody ought to,' retorted Cheryl irritably.

'Oh, for crying out loud, you're about as much fun as a wet week-end in Bootle. I'm sick of everyone getting on my back. Why don't you all just leave me alone?'

Cheryl recognized the mood. There was no talking to Kev once he had turned gangster on you. It was time to backtrack.

'Kev, I ...'

He was obviously in no mood to listen. Digging his fists deep in his trouser pockets he walked moodily alongside her. Brilliant! She'd blown it already. His arrival at Cropper Lane might make her uncomfortable, but she was going to have to live with it.

'Hi there, Cheryl.'

It was Helen, her best friend.

'You must be Kevin,' said the tall, auburn-haired girl.

Kev didn't so much as look at her. Cheryl had a stab at involving him in the conversation. 'Kev, this is Helen. I'm sure I've mentioned her.'

He didn't answer. Sometimes, he was about as charming as a maladjusted piranha.

'Sorry about our Kev,' she whispered as he moved a few paces ahead of them.

'What are you apologizing for?' asked Helen.

Cheryl grimaced. Her friend's voice had that treacly tone to it, the same one she used when Mr Jackson was about.

'Oh, don't tell me you fancy him! Not our Kev.'

Helen gave a mischievous shrug of the shoulders. 'I wouldn't say no to his address,' she chuckled.

'You're welcome to it,' said Cheryl. 'He lives on Owen Avenue.'

'What, *the* Owen Avenue? As in the Diamond estate?'

The mention of one of the roughest streets in the area killed that bit of the conversation stone dead.

'Good week-end?' asked Helen.

'Not bad.'

'We went bowling. You know, the one off the East Lancs. It was great. I thought you might have called round for me.'

'I couldn't. Family ... business.' She had almost said trouble, but Helen didn't seem to have noticed the tell-tale catch in her voice.

'Did you go anywhere?' she asked.

Cheryl shook her head. 'No, we just stayed in.'

And that's all she was going to offer. What Helen would make of the truth she just couldn't imagine. Cheryl wasn't really sure how to handle it herself, and she was family.

'How come he's changed school, anyway?'

'Who?'

'What do you mean, who? Your Kevin, of course.'

'He isn't *my* Kevin.'

'Pardon me for breathing.'

Cheryl sighed. It was apology time. 'Sorry, I didn't mean to snap.'

'As the crocodile said to the swimmer,' Helen joked.

That broke the tension a little, but it did nothing to satisfy Helen's curiosity.

'Well, why did he change school a month into the school year? He didn't get expelled, did he?'

'Don't talk daft.'

'Then what?'

'Nothing, I tell you. They just moved.'

'What, to the Diamond? Nobody *chooses* to live there. Not unless they've had a lobotomy first. I'm right, aren't I? Something happened.'

Cheryl had been anxious about Kev's first day, but she wasn't prepared for anything like this. How could she have been so stupid? She hadn't even worked out a story.

'Nothing happened.'

'Nothing?' Helen repeated dismissively. 'Don't give me that. I'm your best friend, remember. I know when something's up.'

'I can't tell you.'

'But I won't pass it on. You know you can count on me.'

She could count on Helen all right. Count on her to spread it all round school. Count on her to shout it from the rooftops. It wasn't that Helen meant any harm. In most ways, she was about the best friend you could hope for. It's just that she was one blabbermouth. Share a secret with Helen, and you might as well broadcast it on the BBC.

'Please, I am your best mate.'

'It's a family thing. Dead boring. You really wouldn't be interested.'

Helen wasn't convinced. Cheryl could almost see the cogs going round.

'I'll lock it away in the darkest corner of my mind and I'll never ever tell.'

Before she had time to apply the thumbscrews any tighter, there was a commotion around the school gates.

'Oh no, not already.'

'I beg your pardon.'

'It's Kevin,' Cheryl said, grinding her teeth. 'He's discovered Andy Ramage.'

Discovered was hardly the word for it. Kevin had still been in a sulk as he approached the gates. He'd been traipsing in, head down, when Andy stepped into his path.

'You new?' asked Andy.

'What's it to you?' His tone was sullen, but defiant.

'Does he know who he's dealing with?' asked Helen. 'That's Brain Damage Ramage he's talking to.'

'Listen, once our Kev's in a nark, he doesn't care who he's talking to. He'd tell the Prime Minister to sling his hook, Kev would.'

'But you should have warned him,' said Helen. 'Andy will kill him.'

'I wouldn't bet on it,' said Cheryl.

Kevin had begun to shove past Andy, only to be restrained by a hand on his jacket. 'The name's Andy,' said the blond-haired boy.

'Andy Ramage,' his side-kick answered helpfully. Tez Cronin was as wide as he was tall, a product of MacDonald's and Cadbury's – a legend in his own lunch-box. Two things gave his life meaning. Food was one, of course. The other was hanging round Andy Ramage, feeding off his hard man reputation.

'I run a little firm,' Andy continued. 'I offer protection.

'Twenty pence a day,' Tez added. 'And your safety's assured. That's right, isn't it, Andy?'

Kevin ignored Tez completely. 'Are you going to take your mitts off my coat,' he demanded in a low, growling voice, 'or do I have to do it for you ?'

You could almost hear the sharp intake of breath around the school yard. You just didn't talk like that to Andy. Not if you wanted to go home with a full set of teeth.

'You what?'

'What's up?' asked Kevin. 'Deaf as well as stupid?'

'Has he got a death wish?' asked Helen.

The hush that had fallen over the playground would have done justice to a cemetery at midnight.

'Who is this pinhead?' Kevin asked Cheryl.

Andy scowled. 'Do you know him, Tasker?'

'Uh huh,' Cheryl replied without enthusiasm. 'He's my cousin.'

'Then tell him who I am,' Andy advised, loudly enough for the whole yard to hear. Tez looked disappointed. Telling people who Andy was had always been his job. 'And tell him the price has just gone up to fifty p.'

'Forget it,' Kevin told him. 'I'm not going to pay you anything so let me pass.'

'You're asking for a fat lip,' warned Andy.

'No,' Kevin replied coolly, 'I'm asking you to get out of my way.'

'Make me,' smirked Andy.

Kevin turned very slowly until he and Andy were standing toe to toe.

'What?'

'He said: "Make me",' Tez announced, an expectant smile spreading over his broad face.

But that's where the confrontation ended. Without another word, Kevin shot a jab into Andy's chest, winding the taller boy.

'Why, I'll ...'

Whatever Andy had in mind, he didn't get to deliver it. Kevin launched himself forward, his fists thudding mercilessly into Andy's face and temples. Andy tried to recover, shielding his head with his arms but Kevin was on fire. He clipped his reeling opponent a couple of times more before jerking him to attention by the coat collar. With a grunt, Kevin slammed Andy against the wall.

'Listen to me, lame-brain,' he snarled. 'Get in my way again and I'll kill you. Got that?'

Andy's blue eyes filled with horror. He had begun to realise what he was dealing with. It wasn't so much the beating; more the realisation that this new arrival had brought him crashing to earth. In a few dizzy seconds his undisputed rule over the Cropper Lane playground was finished. To all but an astonished Tez and a few of Andy's other cronies, Kevin was an instant hero. Cheryl watched with a sinking heart as kids drifted admiringly in his direction.

'What's your name?' they asked.

'That was brill.'

'Where did you learn to fight like that?'

'Can I be in your gang?'

'You know what?' Helen confided.

'What?'

Cheryl was feeling touchy.

'Your Kevin's made himself number one. Five minutes in the place and he's King Rat already.'

'Rat is about right,' muttered Cheryl.

'What's that supposed to mean?' asked Helen.

'Nothing.'

She bit her lip. Kev's arrival had thrown her into confusion. Even while he had been pummelling Andy into submission, she had been torn. Sure, she'd wanted him to stop. For his own sake, if for no other reason. The one thing he couldn't afford just then was a high profile. But there was something else, something that filled her with guilt. The fight had made her tingle with excitement. Watching Kevin overturn with his fists in one minute everything Brain Damage had spent years building up had thrilled her. That mad, brave, reckless action summed him up. But it was like those action films on Sky; fine to watch, but you wouldn't want to go through it in real life. It was the way he just threw himself into things that excited her. And yet … There was still what she knew about him, and that made her disgusted at her own feelings.

Meanwhile, the tidal wave of adulation continued to engulf Kevin.

'What did you say your name was?'

'McGovern.'

'That's it, then,' said Jamie Moore. We'll call you the Guv'nor.'

'Come with us. We'll show you the ropes.'

'Yes, welcome to Cropper Lane, Guv.'

Mr Jackson appeared at the door. An instant later the shrill blast of his whistle pierced the damp, morning air.

'Get a move on,' he shouted. 'And stop pushing.'

As Cheryl gratefully joined her class's line, she was aware of the other kids jostling to be close to Kevin. He was flavour of the month all right. But for how long?

Two

THIS MORNING BEFORE SCHOOL I STARED UP AT THE sun until it made me go blind. All I could feel was the wind on my face and it was like there was no Liverpool and no Cropper Lane. Just me and the world turning under my feet. I could be anywhere and do anything. I thought maybe when the blackness cleared you would be there. You would have been proud of me today, Dad. I did what you always told me; I got my retaliation in first. No, I didn't pick the fight. It was all Brain Damage's fault. He started it, but I sure finished it.

The trouble is, it doesn't last long, that feeling. I had a real buzz afterwards, but now I feel really low. Don't get me wrong, it isn't Brain Damage that bothers me. I could batter him with one hand tied behind my back. What I'm saying is: I can't afford the aggro. I mean, I know I've been skating on thin ice ever since that old guy. You know what it's like, you get a reputation and everybody's watching you for the slightest little thing.

Just imagine what would happen if Brain Damage ever found out. The only reason I turned him over so easily is because everybody hates him. Jamie Moore – he's my new best mate – and the others have been dying for somebody to knock him off his perch for years. Probably, I was the answer to all their prayers. Do you know what they're calling me now – the Guv'nor. It's a cracking nickname, I like it, but what would happen if they hated me, too? If they ever found

out, I'd be dead meat. Brain Damage and his lousy mates
would take their revenge good style.

Like I said, I'm skating on thin ice.

Three

'**K**EV,' SAID CHERYL.

'That's me,' Kevin acknowledged.

'Do you mind if I walk home with you?'

'Suit yourself,' said Kevin. 'I thought you were getting a lift home with that mate of yours.'

'I was,' Cheryl replied. 'We were going to offer you one, too. Didn't you notice? She had to leave early. Her dad came in half-way through the club.'

'Did he? I wasn't paying much attention.'

'That was pretty obvious,' Cheryl snorted. 'It was embarrassing. Everybody noticed. Can't you at least *try* to be enthusiastic?'

'Why should I?'

'Oh, I don't know.' Cheryl thought for a minute, then continued. 'By the way, what was Helen saying to you when we first got there? You know, when I was talking to Karen Jarman.'

'Curious, are you?' Kevin asked with a mischievous glint in his eye.

'Not particularly.' But she was lying through her teeth and he knew it.

'She invited me to tea,' he announced triumphantly. He enjoyed putting Cheryl's nose out of joint.

'She what?'

'Invited me to tea. Tomorrow night.'

'But she's coming to mine tomorrow!'

'You'd better tell her that,' chuckled Kevin, revelling in Cheryl's discomfort. 'Anyway, I told her I couldn't go. To be honest, I don't want to.'

Cheryl was stunned. How could her best mate treat her like that?

'That was a waste of an hour, wasn't it?' said Kevin.

'The High School Club? I thought it was really good.'

'You would. What's so good about it?'

He glared at the gates of the Scarisbrick High. It was a new idea that had started that term. The Year Six kids were encouraged to attend a fortnightly club after school to get them used to the High School they would be attending the following autumn. Cheryl was excited about it. Needless to say, Kevin wasn't. If his mother hadn't frog-marched him in, he would never have come.

Cheryl shook her head. She was still smarting over Helen's behaviour. 'You wouldn't understand.'

'Who wants to?' grumbled Kevin.

Cheryl turned up her coat collar against the biting wind. Some company he was going to be.

'Anyway,' said Kevin. 'Are we going to make a move, or what?'

'Might as well,' said Cheryl. 'It doesn't look like it's going to let up.'

She watched the clouds of fine rain drifting across the waste-ground opposite. Scarisbrick lay on the west side of the Diamond estate where Kevin lived. The Northern Line railway whose lights were beginning to glimmer dimly in the distance divided the Diamond from the neat turn-of the-century houses Cheryl called home.

The two areas were no more than five minutes' walk apart, but it may as well have been a hundred miles. In Cheryl's settled neighbourhood almost everybody was working, but on the Diamond, jobs were rarer than a polar bear in the tropics.

'I bet Helen was looking forward to the drive home tonight,' said Cheryl, a spiteful edge creeping into her voice.

'Meaning?'

'Oh nothing.'

'Go on, spit it out.'

'Meaning she's got her eye on you. I think she fancies you.'

'Got good taste then, hasn't she?' said Kevin.

'Think so, do you?'

'Is that the way home?' asked Kevin, pointing across the waste-ground.

'Yes, but Mum doesn't let me go that way. She prefers me to walk the long way round.'

Kevin didn't care what Cheryl's mum preferred. Without a word, he stepped out into the rain and set off briskly towards the railway line.

'Hey,' Cheryl cried. 'Which way do you think you're going?'

'The short-cut, the one you told me about yesterday. You can go the long way round if you want.'

Tying her hood under her chin, Cheryl made after him.

'I hope you know I'm wearing my best trainers.'

'It's all right if you've got best trainers,' Kevin retorted sourly.

Aunt Carol did her best, but her benefit didn't allow for many luxuries. Most of the time, Kev and his little brother Gareth had to make do with the cheap brands of everything. And, to make things worse, Cheryl's eleventh birthday was coming up shortly. One look at her presents, and Kevin would be more prickly than ever.

'Oh, this is stupid,' Cheryl complained, as she slithered clumsily across the muddy ground.

'I didn't ask you to follow me,' said Kevin.

'Just imagine what Aunt Carol would think if I didn't,' Cheryl answered. She knew it was the wrong thing to mention, but she said it nonetheless. The news about Helen inviting him to tea had got under her skin.

'Are you telling me my mum asked you to spy on me?'

'Not in so many words.'

'But that's what she meant.'

'My mum and yours thought it would be a good idea for us to come back together, that's all. I was supposed to look out for you. I couldn't care less, but Helen obviously does.'

Kevin's features twisted. A hawk who could kill. 'I knew it. I thought it was too good to be true when Mum said I could walk home on my own. She knew you and Helen would be waiting.'

Cheryl remembered the phone conversation between her mother and Aunt Carol the night before. They must have spent half an hour discussing how best to keep him out of trouble.

'Well, they can forget it!' Kevin announced suddenly. Without further ado, he took off towards the railway line.

'Kevin!'

Cheryl was almost crying. There, in the middle of the waste-ground where the rubber factory had once been, she felt alone and scared. The darkness was closing round her like a fist. This raw wilderness was where youths off the Diamond drove robbed cars and set them alight, and where the local gangs gathered to settle their differences. It was the tortured heart of the whole district. It was, in short, completely off-limits. Cheryl screwed her eyes tight. Why, oh why did Helen have to go early?

'Just wait till you want some help off me, you tight pig!'

The words were meant as a reprimand, but they came out as a thin bleat of fear, and evaporated mournfully into the evening air.

'Just wait,' she murmured nervously.

After some hesitation, Cheryl opted to follow Kevin on to the muddy path that ran along the Northern Line in the hope he might relent and wait for her.

'Mum would kill me if she knew I'd come down here after dark,' she told herself in a quavering voice.

Ahead of her lay a litter of broken paving stones and abandoned oil drums. Broken glass gleamed under the railway lighting. It gave her the creeps. She was about to call after Kevin when she caught sight of him, a stark figure etched against the gloom.

'Kev—'

Her voice broke off. She had suddenly distinguished two shadowy figures facing him, and as she drew closer, she recognized them.

'Ramage.'

Tez wasn't even worth the breath it took to say his name. Within seconds of Cheryl recognizing the boys, the sound of an angry exchange reached her ears.

'We thought it was you,' said Andy. 'We couldn't believe our luck when we saw you coming, could we, Tez?'

Tez gave a humourless chuckle. 'That's when we planned this little ambush,' he said.

'So where do you think you're going now, McGovern?' Andy demanded.

'None of your business, Brain Damage,' Kevin replied.

That brought Andy up short. He nearly choked at the mention of his nickname. It might be what everybody at Cropper Lane called him, but not to his face.

'Where did you hear that?'

Kevin smiled. 'Wouldn't you like to know?'

Andy's eyes were blazing. 'I think it's time you paid for that lucky punch yesterday morning.'

Kevin raised an eyebrow. 'Is that what you call it, lucky?'

'Like to try me again?'

'Behave,' said Kevin. 'I'd batter you.'

'Think so, do you?'

With that, Andy threw a punch, but Kevin side-stepped it.

'You'll have to do better than that.'

Andy tried, but his clumsy charge was easily dealt with. Kevin stepped aside and cuffed him sharply across the side of the head. With a yelp of surprise, Andy stumbled to the ground.

'Like I said,' Kevin hissed. 'Behave yourself.'

Andy tried to rise, but was shoved off balance by a sharp toe poke from Kev's trainer. Tez shaped up half-heartedly to defend his friend. Without the rest of the gang, he was more a cheer-leader than a fighter.

'You want some as well, do you?' Kevin asked in a voice full of menace.

Tez hesitated.

'Well?'

The moment had passed. Tez lowered his eyes in an admission of defeat.

'I thought you'd see it my way,' said Kevin. 'Come on, Cheryl. The way's clear.'

Cheryl joined him gratefully. 'But how did you know I was there?'

'Peripheral vision.'

'What?'

'Something Dad taught me. If you're a fighter, you've got to know what's coming at you.'

At the mention of her Uncle Tony, Cheryl felt a pang of unease. A fighter wasn't what her mother called him. Low-life was her usual term.

'You still think about your dad, don't you, Kev?'

He was taking the steps which led from the railway path to the main road.

'Of course I do. He's my dad.'

He sure is, thought Cheryl. Maybe that's half the trouble.

Four

'HAT YOU, CHERYL?'
'Yes.'

Her mother poked her head round the living room door, her eyes alighting immediately on Cheryl's muddy trainers.

'What on earth ...?'

'Kev wanted to cut across the waste-ground.'

'And you had to follow, I suppose?'

Cheryl nodded. That's when the penny dropped with Mum.

'Just a minute. Waste-ground? You mean you came home the back way. In the dark!'

'Sorry.'

'So you should be. How many times do your dad and I have to warn you about things like that?'

Here it comes, thought Cheryl, the third degree.

'And how come you didn't get a lift? Wasn't Helen there tonight?'

'Yes, but something happened. Her gran's had a fall.'

Mum devoted the next couple of minutes to expressions of concern about Helen's gran, but she soon returned to carping on about the risk Cheryl had taken coming home the back way.

'Do you know how worried I've been? I expected you half an hour ago. I was about to ring Helen's mum.'

'But what could I do, Mum? Helen had gone and Kev

—— 19 ——

was hanging round. I thought you'd want me to stick with him.'

Her mother softened. 'Yes, you're right of course. You're a sensible girl, Cheryl, which is more than I can say for your dad.'

'Why, what's he done?'

'That's just it. Nothing.'

'What do you mean?'

'Two hours late, he is. No warning, no phone call, nothing. I've been climbing the walls. You start imagining all sorts.'

'You don't think he's had an accident, do you?' Cheryl asked.

'I hope not.'

Cheryl gave her mother an anxious look.

'Oh, I didn't mean to worry you. I'm sure he's all right. He's invincible, your dad. What's Kevin been up to, anyway?'

Cheryl considered telling the truth, but thought better of it. Mum had flipped enough over her taking a short cut. Goodness only knows what she'd make of the confrontation with Brain Damage.

'He took off on me, that's all.'

'Why, have you two been arguing?'

'No, not really. You know Kev.'

'Yes,' her mother said wryly. 'I know Kev, all right. I don't half feel sorry for our Carol. First, Tony clears off on her, then all this bother with Kev. I don't know how she copes, honestly I don't.'

The answer, thought Cheryl, is not very well. Mum and Aunt Carol were twin sisters, but you would never imagine it. Aunt Carol looked a good five years older. Her face was drawn, and she had dark lines round her eyes. You could even see it in her hair. It was dull, lifeless somehow. She chain-smoked, too. All the worry, Mum said.

'Mum,' Cheryl began hesitantly.

'Yes?'

'Why was Aunt Carol crying yesterday?'

'You heard, did you?'

'I couldn't help it. She was really upset, wasn't she?'

'Oh, she was upset, all right. Kev's been knocking round with that lad again.'

'Rooster?'

Cheryl's mum sighed. 'Yes, that's right, Rooster.'

Rooster had been Kevin's best mate on the old estate. He was a pasty-looking, red-haired boy. Hence Rooster, as in Little Red. He was no hard-case. In a way he was more dangerous than that. Sly and underhand, he contrived to manufacture trouble, but he never seemed to be around to face the music.

'Kev went missing at tea-time,' her mother told her. 'He took money out of Carol's purse and sloped off by himself. He was away hours. She was going spare. That's why she came round here. She was thinking of calling the police.'

'So how did she find him?'

'Your dad drove her down to look for him. We had a good idea where Kev would be. He can't seem to leave his old stamping ground behind. Twenty minutes on the bus and he still goes sneaking back. That's why she made him go to that after-school club tonight. Keep him out of mischief.'

Cheryl avoided any mention of what had really happened after the club. She didn't want her voice to give her away.

'No wonder she was so upset,' she said. 'I hate Rooster. He makes my flesh creep.'

'I should think so. He's a right tearaway, that one. Reminds me a bit of Kev's dad.'

'Poor Aunt Carol,' said Cheryl.

'Half of it's down to that no-good Tony McGovern. Fancy deserting your family. I was lucky meeting a good, steady fellow like your dad. There but for fortune.'

Cheryl gave a slight shudder. It was her mother's final words that bothered her, the idea that something could just happen to you; something sudden and terrible and as much a matter of chance as the throw of a dice. Compared to Kevin's, her life seemed so good; so cosy and predictable. She was an only child and she got most of the things she wanted, an Amiga, a CD player, holidays abroad, the best labels on her trainers and clothes. Most of all, she had the security of a mum and dad who loved the bones of her and spoilt her rotten. OK, from time to time Kev's escapades held a strange fascination for her, but she wouldn't change places for the world. She liked Dad's explanation of things; that you get what you deserve in this world. Surely that was exactly how it should be. Work hard and keep out of trouble and everything will be fine. Yes, that's how it had to be. Kev was proof of it, but in reverse. If only he could steer clear of bother.

'What if we didn't have my dad?'

'What a funny question!'

'But what if we didn't?'

'We'd get by. Lots of women do. I've got my job, too, remember, and even if I didn't it wouldn't be the end of the world.'

'It would be hard, though,' Cheryl objected. 'Kev's always moaning that he doesn't get things bought for him.'

'That isn't fair,' her mother answered. 'Carol's a good

mother, you know. She doesn't spend a penny on herself. The odd ciggy's her only pleasure.'

The *odd* ciggy, Cheryl thought, that's a laugh.

'Everything goes on the kids,' Mum continued. 'Just imagine if her Tony was still around. He's never done a proper day's work in his life. He was always up to some scam or other. Kev would be even more of a handful looking up to somebody like that. Believe you me, they're better off without a dad than with one like him.'

Cheryl tried to picture her uncle, but the best she could manage was a hazy image of an unshaven, hard-looking man in a leather bomber jacket. His dark features stayed in Cheryl's memory. That was where Kevin got his looks. Three years had erased almost everything else. About the only thing she could remember was the way Dad was always calling him a waste of space. That was the tag they hung on him – the good-for-nothing, the villain.

'But was he like that in the beginning? You know, when they first got married. He must have cared once.'

Her mother was twitching at the curtains, gazing down the rain-swept street for some sign of the car.

'Tony? Handsome as they come, but a nasty piece of work.' She paused, as if reconsidering. 'Oh, I don't know, maybe life never gave him much of a chance. Mind you, I can't say I took to the lad, myself. Never did understand what our Carol saw in him. She had enough fellows running after her when she was younger. Why she settled for Tony, I'll never know.'

'That's what you always say,' Cheryl complained. 'But what was it about him? Why didn't you like him?'

'Because he let our Carol down, that's why.'

Cheryl knew she was being fobbed off.

'But—'

'Here he is,' her mother said as Dad's car drew up. Before Cheryl could say another word, Mum was heading for the front door. 'About time, too!' she declared. 'I'll wipe the floor with him.'

Her mother always said something like that when she was worried. If she didn't have her little rant, she would just dissolve into floods of tears. Cheryl listened to the sounds of conversation from the hall, loud at first then softer. The exchange lasted a few moments then there was silence. That's what rang the alarm bells. The few times her father had been late before, it had sparked a sharp argument, especially when Mum was due at work. But not this time.

'Hi, Dad,' said Cheryl, walking into the hallway.

Her father was still standing on the step. He didn't answer. He was wearing a strange expression, as if he was bewildered and embarrassed, the victim of some silly practical joke. Maybe if he'd had chocolate sauce trickling down his face it would have been funny. Instead, it was deeply unsettling. Invincible he definitely wasn't.

'What is it?' asked Cheryl, her stomach clenching. 'What's wrong?'

Her parents exchanged glances.

'It's your dad,' Mum replied. 'He's just been made redundant.'

Cheryl stared at her father.

'It's simple,' he explained, taking her look as an unspoken question. 'Ninety days from now, I won't have a job any more. Wonderful, eh? Two months before Christmas, and this is the news we get.'

As he edged past and hung up his coat, four words haunted her; *there but for fortune*.

The following morning found Cheryl in the corner of the playground. She was confiding in Helen, all the while compulsively twisting her hair.

'What's up with you pair?' came a voice.

Cheryl looked up, but Helen was the first to respond to Kevin's question. 'You mean you don't know? It's her dad, he's lost his job.'

'When?'

'I found out last night,' Cheryl answered. 'They had this big meeting at work. They read out a list; who was going and who was staying, and my dad's got the push.'

'How come?'

'Don't ask me. He was going on about it all last night. Something about picking out the blue-eyed boys.'

'So what does that mean?'

'How should I know?'

Cheryl was feeling sore. She'd been sent to bed early so that her parents could talk. She'd lain awake for hours listening to the dull rhythm of their voices drifting up through the floor. As if it didn't affect her, too!

'He'll get another job,' said Kevin nonchalantly.

'Oh, you know that, do you?' Cheryl was offended. How dare he treat it so lightly? Her dad had been shattered by the news, and Kev was acting as if it didn't matter one bit.

'All right, keep your hair on.'

Glancing self-consciously at the finger twiddling her hair, she let her hand drop.

Helen intervened to calm things down. 'Is *your* dad working, Kev?'

'No,' he told her, before adding the hurried qualification, 'But he's gone down South ... for an interview.'

His eyes met Cheryl's, willing her not to say anything.

'Brain Damage has been quiet, hasn't he?' Kevin went on, changing the subject.

'Not half,' said Helen. 'You were brilliant the other day. It looked like you knew what you were doing.'

Kevin was basking in the admiration. 'I can handle myself. My dad was … is a boxer.'

'Really,' cooed Helen. 'I thought it must be something like that.'

'It was only a playground fight.' grumbled Cheryl. Helen's adulation was getting a bit hard to take. It was getting embarrassing.

'Only!' Helen protested. 'So how come nobody else has ever stood up to Andy? Tell me that.'

'Anyway,' said Kevin. 'You don't know the half of it.'

It was Cheryl's turn to flash a silent message with her eyes. He couldn't reveal his secret, not like this.

'You mean there's more?' asked Helen.

'Are you going to tell her, Cheryl, or shall I?'

Cheryl was flustered. 'I don't …'

'Last night,' Kevin reminded her. 'The ambush.'

'Oh that.' Relief flooded through her.

'Well?' Helen asked breathlessly. 'Give, will you. What's the big secret?'

'Brain Damage was waiting for Kev after the High School Club. Him and Tez jumped us on the railway path.'

'So what happened?'

'Kev decked Brain Damage.'

'You never!'

'I did.'

'And Tez?'

'He bottled it,' Kevin answered scornfully. 'They were a pushover.'

'I wish I'd been there,' said Helen.

Cheryl was feeling almost physically sick. This was turning into hero-worship and Kev was lapping it up. The next thing she knew, he would be taking up Helen's offer of tea at her house.

'What about my dad?' she asked irritably.

Helen looked confused. 'What about your dad?'

'I was telling you about him, remember.'

With that, she marched away across the yard and hung around the railings, feeling utterly miserable. She could see Kevin and Helen. They were talking animatedly. She might as well be invisible. As she watched Helen drooling over Kev, she felt angry and frustrated. Whose friend was she, anyway? It was while she stood kicking her heels by the railings that she noticed Brain Damage. He was crossing the yard, accompanied by Tez and another of his cronies.

'Now I wonder what you're up to?' Cheryl thought aloud.

It wasn't long before she found out. They cornered Bashir, a Year Five boy who'd started six months earlier. His family were refugees and he still didn't speak English that well.

'Hey,' Andy shouted. 'We want a word with you.'

'I don't want no trouble,' said Bashir in his gruff, heavily-accented voice.

'And you won't get any,' said Andy. 'So long as you pay up.'

'No money,' said Bashir. 'Since you take it all, my mother don't give me none.'

'That right?' asked Andy, running his finger down Bashir's cheek. 'Well, you just listen to me, if you don't have at least a couple of quid for me by the end of the week, I'm going to take it out of your black skin. Got that?'

Bashir simply stared back.

'I said, got that?'

Andy accompanied the question with a jarring slap to the side of Bashir's head.

'Yes.'

'Good. You make sure you've got my money.'

The three boys wandered back across the yard.

'Are you all right?' Cheryl asked as Bashir rubbed his temple.

'Yes, I'm all right.'

'You ought to tell the teacher.'

Bashir shook his head. 'I will pay.'

'I think you're wrong,' said Cheryl. 'It only encourages them.'

'You don't get hit,' Bashir answered ruefully.

Before she could say another word, the bell rang; dinner-time break was over. As she joined Year Six J's line, Cheryl heard Helen's voice behind her.

'What got into you?'

'Sorry,' said Cheryl, keen to avoid an argument. 'It's all this with my dad.'

'Kev says it'll be all right.'

'So what does he know?' Cheryl snapped. 'If he's so great, how come Andy's still bullying? I thought the Guv'nor' – she spat the word sarcastically – 'I thought the Guv'nor had got it sorted.'

'Have you heard this, Kev?' asked Helen. 'Tell him, Cher.'

'It's Andy,' Cheryl explained. 'He's been having a go at one of the kids in Y5. His name's Bashir. You ought to know him. He lives on Owen Avenue, same as you. The top end, somewhere. Andy's demanding money off him.'

'Is he now?' Kevin looked across in Andy's direction.

'It'll take more than a punch in the face to stop Andy,' said Cheryl. 'Bully's his middle name.'

'You may just be right,' said Kevin thoughtfully. 'I'll have to see what I can come up with.'

Five

*Y*OU KNOW SOMETHING, DAD, I MIGHT JUST HAVE *it. So they want me to be the Guv'nor, do they? I've got a whole bunch of new mates and I'm the boss. Well, I might give them more than they bargained for. Weeks I've been keeping my head down. Not any more. I'll make them sit up and take notice. I'm starting to feel like I'm in charge again.*

It was Brain Damage who gave me the idea. He runs this little protection racket in school. Not much. Just loose change, really, ten pence here, twenty there, but he scares some of the younger kids out of their wits. To be honest, I thought he'd have the sense to stop after our last run-in. It seems he's thicker-skinned than I thought, or maybe just plain thicker! Anyway, I know exactly what to do. I'm going to sort things. It's boss, isn't it? Just think of it, Mum's always saying I ought to be good. Well, what could be better? They'll be calling me Robin Hood next.

You just wait. Next time he so much as comes near, I'll have him. Wherever he goes, whatever he does, I'm going to be on his case. I'm going to haunt him. I'll be his worst nightmare. And you know what? I'm not even going to use my fists. I've got a far better plan. I've put out the feelers and everybody I've mentioned it to loves my idea. I'm looking forward to this. You know what Brain Damage is? He's my passport to power. So that's it, Dad. Good, isn't it? I knew you'd be proud of me.

Six

IT WAS THREE DAYS LATER THAT KEVIN REALLY made his name as the Guv with a capital G. Thinking back, what was to so incense Cheryl was that she seemed to be the last person to know what he was up to. He had drawn just about everybody else into his confidence. It must have taken some planning too, *days* of it. There had been inklings of what was to come all day. For starters, Jacko had caught Danny Stone with a packet of wallpaper paste in his bag, but Danny hadn't let on what it was for. Not even when he had to stay in all playtime because of it. Then, just before morning break, Cheryl had seen Kevin displaying a tin of custard powder to a giggling posse of his new admirers, one of them holding a jar of marmalade. It was, however, only when she heard on the grapevine that Jamie Moore had brought in an inflatable paddling pool that she really became suspicious. Jamie and Kev had become inseparable at school and they were definitely up to something.

'Hey, Cheryl,' Helen called as they filed out of class. 'Guess what I've just heard.'

'I don't know. What?'

'Just a minute. Let them go past first.'

She meant Year Six H. There were two top junior classes at Cropper Lane. Cheryl, Kevin and Helen were in Year Six J. Andy Ramage and Tez were in Year Six H, which is why Helen was keeping quiet until they'd gone.

'It's Brain Damage,' Helen continued once the coast was clear. 'Kev's planning a little surprise for him.'

Cheryl felt a tug of apprehension. 'What sort of surprise?'

'Andy will be after that Somali kid at home-time for his protection money.'

'You mean Bashir?'

'Yes, and that's when Brain Damage gets it.'

'Gets what?'

'I'm not quite sure. Girls aren't supposed to be in on this. But it's big. Come on, or we'll miss it.'

Cheryl had never seen the classroom empty so quickly. She could tell that Mr Jackson was bemused by the stampede. Kev and Jamie Moore had been the first out of the door. 'I don't like the sound of this,' she murmured. 'I just hope Kev knows what he's doing.'

As they reached the school gates, Helen tapped Cheryl on the shoulder. 'Look over there.'

Jamie was carrying the paddling pool, now fully inflated, towards the park opposite school. He was being followed by three other boys.

'Is that for Andy?'

'What do you think?'

The slight anxiety she had been feeling all day had suddenly turned into a rush of overwhelming panic. Somebody was going to get into trouble, and if it was Kevin, she'd be dragged down with him.

'Helen, are you sure you don't know more than you're telling?'

'All I know is it's going to sort out Brain Damage for good. Look, it's starting.'

Helen was nodding in the direction of Bashir. He was trying to slip unseen out of school.

'Where do you think you're going?' came a loud voice.

It belonged to Andy Ramage.

'I'm going home.'

'Haven't you forgotten something?' Andy asked.

Bashir kept quiet, his eyes trained steadfastly on the ground ahead of him.

'If I didn't know better,' Andy told Tez, tagging along as usual, 'I'd think Bashir here has been avoiding me.'

'Surely not,' smirked Tez.

'Anyway,' Andy continued, the smile fading from his face. 'Where's my money?'

'I couldn't get it,' confessed Bashir.

'Couldn't get it, eh?' said Andy. 'Well, I told you what would happen if you didn't.'

'Why doesn't somebody do something?' said Cheryl. 'You know where they're going to take him.'

Helen knew, of course, and so did poor Bashir. Everyone in the school knew exactly what was in store if you got the wrong side of Andy. You'd be dragged into the park and battered, and probably shoved into the lake for good measure.

Helen waited until Andy and Tez had wrestled the struggling Bashir across the road and into the park. 'Come on,' she said excitedly.

The three boys had just reached the flower beds on the far side of the park lake when Kevin appeared. He wasn't alone. At his side stood Jamie Moore and eight or nine other boys.

'What do you want?' asked Andy.

Kevin smiled. 'You.'

'Get knotted.'

The words were defiant, but they were delivered in a voice that was shaking audibly.

'Clear off, Tez,' Kevin ordered. 'We don't need you. We only want Brain Damage.'

Tez glanced nervously at Andy. He dithered for a few

moments, then gratefully detached himself from Andy and hurried away.

While Tez was making for home, Cheryl became aware of more kids arriving. They were looking forward to the big show.

'Now,' said Kevin. 'Be a good little boy Brain Damage. Let him go.'

Andy released Bashir then made a run for it. He had barely gone five steps before he was bundled roughly to the ground by Kevin and Jamie.

'Oh no you don't,' said Kevin. 'Right lads, truss him up.'

Andy's hands were quickly bound with cord and a handkerchief stuffed unceremoniously into his mouth. His eyes were staring as he struggled.

'Now,' said Kevin. 'It's about time you got a taste of your own medicine, Brain Damage.'

As he twisted against their restraining hands, Andy spat out the handkerchief. 'I'll get you back for this, McGovern.'

Kevin shook his head. 'No, you won't. Right lads, gunge him.'

At last, Cheryl understood. The paddling pool was full to the brim with a thick, stomach-turning mess.

'What's in it?' Helen asked the nearest boy. 'Besides the paste and the custard.'

'Everybody brought something,' he answered. 'Eggs, sour milk, oil, all sorts.' He lowered his voice. 'Jamie brought the best, though.'

'What's that?'

'Oh, just a little something his grandad puts on his allotment.'

Cheryl and Helen must still have looked puzzled.

'You know, it comes out of the back end of a horse.'

'Oh, gross!'

Kevin was basking in the attention his plan had brought.

'Now!' he cried.

As Andy was dragged closer to the paddling pool Jamie started a chant. 'Gunge him! Gunge him!'

It was soon taken up by the rest of the Cropper Lane kids. 'Gunge him. Gunge him. Gunge him!'

Kevin was left to administer the last push. With a cry of helpless rage, Andy fell face first into the foul mixture. After that, the game was open to all comers. At least a dozen boys and girls were surrounding the paddling pool, making sure that Andy didn't escape. Time and again he struggled to his feet only to be thrown back into the clinging mess.

For all her reservations, even Cheryl found herself roaring with laughter along with the rest.

'Gunge him. Gunge him!' she shouted as mud and rotting leaves were added to the concoction that was plastered all over Andy's hair, face and uniform.

'Gunge him!'

It was then that she remembered Bashir. He was standing just behind her, watching the mêlée. 'What do you think, Bashir?'

'I think Brain Damage will hurt me for this.'

'Don't be daft,' said Helen. 'Kev's sorted him out good style. He did it for you.'

Bashir's brown eyes were expressionless. Very slowly and deliberately, he shook his head.

'What's that supposed to mean?' Helen demanded. 'Of course he did it for you.'

'No,' said Bashir, turning to leave. 'He did it for himself.'

'Well!' Helen exclaimed indignantly. 'Would you believe that? There's no pleasing some people.'

Cheryl turned to watch Kevin. He was standing on a

log, waving a stick and leading the chants of: 'Gunge him! Gunge him!'

'Bashir's right,' she said. The boy's words were like a flash of lightning, making everything crystal clear 'You idiot,' she went on under her breath. Did he want to draw attention to himself? Did he really want everything to come out? It was as if Kevin was asking to be found out. HMS Kev was heading for the rocks, and if he went down, lifeboat Cheryl was sure to sink with him. One thing was obvious, if she was to save the comfy little life she had, she would have to save Kevin, too.

'Oh, you've just got a downer on him,' said Helen.

Cheryl rolled her eyes. 'You don't know anything.'

'Maybe you ought to tell me, then. What is this big secret of Kev's?'

'Don't be stupid,' Cheryl answered. You're not going to find out, she told herself, *nobody* is. Without another word, she strode across the grass and planted herself between Andy and his tormentors. If Kevin didn't have the sense to keep out of trouble, she did. There's nothing like the threat of disaster for giving you courage.

'Let him go,' she cried.

'Get out of the way,' shouted Jamie Moore. 'Girls shouldn't be here, anyway.'

Cheryl glared at Kevin, challenging him to intervene. 'Tell them, Kev.'

Her words were brave, but inside she was feeling sick.

'Well, Guv?' asked Jamie.

Kevin looked deflated. Because it was so unexpected, Cheryl's outburst had twice the impact.

'You can let him go,' he sighed.

Andy stepped out of the paddling pool and immediately slipped on the slimy grass. As he lay flat on his back, he looked a pathetic figure. Raucous laughter greeted his attempts to get to his feet. Two boys started to pelt him with clods of earth. But Cheryl put a stop to that. She stepped in the way, making herself Andy's shield. She knew she wasn't doing it for the forlorn bully slithering miserably on the grass, but for herself and for Kevin. She had a mission. She was going to save them both. From *the secret* and what would happen if it got out.

'Leave him alone,' she shrieked.

Again, the questioning looks in Kevin's direction. Kevin nodded. It looked like at long last he'd remembered he was still skating on thin ice. Maybe her plan had a chance.

Andy finally succeeded in standing and began to walk away, the mixture running in thick gobs down his clothes. The crowd was starting to disperse when he turned.

'I'll get you, McGovern. No matter what it takes, I'm going to get even.'

The threat from such a comic figure simply set off more laughter. But Cheryl didn't join in. She had seen Andy's eyes. She had seen the hatred. It was no idle threat.

Seven

I KNOW YOU'RE NOT GOING TO BELIEVE THIS, DAD, BUT I *didn't enjoy today. Mad, isn't it? There I am, cock of the school and I wind up feeling totally depressed.*

It wouldn't have even occurred to me if Cheryl hadn't stuck in her two pennyworth. I wonder what got into her today? Usually, she wouldn't say boo to a goose. Suddenly she's shouting the odds at the lot of us. I mean, I was finding it pretty easy to treat Brain Damage like the animal he is until she spoke up. The trouble is, the moment I heard her yelling at everyone like that, I could suddenly see myself in his place.

I know you'll think I'm going soft, but I've been there, remember. I spent weeks on the receiving end. It's not that I feel sorry for Brain Damage. He deserves everything he gets. No, it was the idea that it could happen to me again. I'll never forget summer, when they drove us off the estate. I'll never forget the icy stares I got after it happened, or the way they kicked lumps out of me.

Mum says it was even worse for her. She was so ashamed when the police came round the house. None of the neighbours would even talk to her. Then there was the social worker asking us all sorts of pointless questions. Willy's like a dog with a bone. She wasn't satisfied with making my life a misery, she had to have a go at Mum as well. That hurt, the way Mum would stare at me like I'd destroyed her life, the way she would cry all the time and say I was throwing away my future. But it wasn't my fault. It was an accident. I never tried to hurt anybody. It's not fair the way I get blamed. You should see Mum. She's just so bitter. She's always having a go at me. Gareth's this good and that good. Me? I'm just a no-good scally.

So that's the upshot of it all, a double whammy. First I get it in the neck for what I've done. I lose my mates, I get battered, everybody points at me in the street and at school. But that's not all. I can't even get away from it at home. That's where Mum starts on at me because of all the grief she's getting from the school and from Willy. Willy's one pain in the neck. Just when Mum's starting to lighten up, around comes Willy to stir it all up again. She arrived on the doorstep tonight. Back off holiday in Cyprus. You should have seen her tan. You could mix gravy with it. 'You didn't get that on Southport beach,' I told her. She just smiled. As usual. Sometimes, I think she's a bit simple, old Willy, or maybe they're told to behave that way. The other social worker was just the same, grinning at me like a Cheshire cat. Doesn't stop them prying, though, does it? To them, you're not a human being, you're a case – a head-case. She asked me all sorts tonight, trying to sound like she cared. I got her, though. She asked me what films I liked. You know what I said: 'Free Willy'. Free Willy with every box of Corn Flakes. Somehow, I don't think she found that too funny. Still, it got rid of her and that's all that matters. You know the trouble with Willy? She lives in some big house in Cheshire or somewhere like that. She hasn't got a clue what it's like for somebody like me. Nobody knows what it's like.

You should have been here for me, Dad. None of this would ever have happened if you hadn't cleared off on us. Where are you? Why did you leave us?

Oh, this is stupid. Who am I kidding? You're not coming back, are you? I've got to face it alone. Still, I'll tell you one thing: I'm never going to let them hurt me again.

I'd die first.

Eight

KEVIN LOOKED UP AT THE SOUND OF THE BACK door opening. 'Oh, it's you.'

'Who did you expect, the flipping Queen?'

Kevin was sprinkling the floor of the guinea pig's hutch with sawdust. 'What got into you yesterday?'

Cheryl shrugged her shoulders.

'Anyway, don't just stand there,' said Kevin. 'Pass me some fresh straw.'

Cheryl obliged.

'You think what I did was wrong, then?' Kevin asked.

'Don't you?'

'Ramage is a nerd.'

'So? That's not the point. It's you I'm worried about, not him.'

'Meaning?'

'He's a bad enemy.'

'I can handle him.'

'In a fight maybe,' Cheryl sighed. 'But couldn't you have sorted things out with Brain Damage without this? You're only going to make things worse.'

'Funny, I thought I was making them better.'

'Oh sure.'

What was wrong with Kevin? He didn't seem to *want* to be saved.

'Anyway,' Kevin added. 'Don't you get on your high horse. I saw you laughing like the rest of us.'

'You're right, I laughed. It was Bashir who changed my mind.'

'Bashir?'

'He seemed really upset by it.'

'You sure?'

Cheryl nodded.

'I give up,' said Kevin. 'Ramage needed sorting.'

'Yes,' Cheryl declared, 'And you had to be the one to do it, didn't you?'

'Oh, I get it.'

'Get what?'

Kevin picked up Domino, his black and white guinea pig, and lowered him into the hutch. 'I might have guessed,' he said. 'I know what's eating you.'

'Are you going to start speaking English?'

'I've just realised what you're getting on your high horse about. I'm embarrassing you. Miss Goody Two Shoes has got a delinquent cousin, and you think school might find out.'

'Don't be stupid.'

'I'm not. That's exactly what you're thinking.'

'I'm not thinking anything of the sort.'

'Oh no? Then why are you blushing?'

Cheryl's hand darted instinctively to her face. 'OK, but I wouldn't have to feel this way if you could behave yourself for five minutes at a stretch. I thought you were going to keep your head down at Cropper Lane.'

'Brain Damage picked on me, remember.'

'You could have walked away.'

'I'm no coward.'

'You're pathetic. You'll end up just like your dad.'

The words were hardly out of her mouth when Cheryl felt a hot surge down her neck and back. She couldn't have said anything crueller if she'd tried.

'Shut up!' Kevin yelled. His face was bulging with a

ferocious anger. 'Shut your mouth. What do you know about my dad?'

'Kev, I'm sorry. I didn't mean it. It just came out.'

'Get lost. Just clear off out of my sight.'

'Kev—'

He started shoving her roughly towards the house. 'Get out of my sight!' He was raging, quite beside himself.

'Kev, you're scaring me.'

'You ever say his name again and I'll kill you. I'll kill you.'

That did it. Cheryl dissolved into tears and fled into the house, leaving Kevin to his fury.

'Cheryl,' her mother said when she burst into the kitchen. 'Whatever's happened?'

Aunt Carol looked up. 'Has our Kev done something?'

Distraught as she was, Cheryl wasn't about to land Kevin in it. 'No, I trapped my finger in the lid of the hutch.'

'Let's see.'

'There's no need. It's feeling better already.'

'Are you telling the truth?' Aunt Carol demanded. 'If this is Kevin's doing, I'll throttle him. I've had enough aggravation off that boy of mine to last a lifetime.'

'No, honestly,' Cheryl answered. 'I hurt myself, that's all.'

It was obvious that nobody believed her.

'Anyway,' said her mother. 'We'd better make tracks. I only wanted to drop off that knitting pattern.'

Cheryl's head snapped round. Knitting pattern? She'd never seen Aunt Carol knitting. Then she saw the real reason for the visit. There was a crisp ten pound note on the table. Mum was lending Aunt Carol money again. Cheryl wondered what it was this time: a new pair of shoes for Gareth, the gas bill or just help with the groceries. Dad would go mad if he knew. He had this thing about lending money. Stops people standing on their own two feet, he said.

'I'd better get home in time for Dave,' Mum continued. 'It's this redundancy business. He's taking it badly.'

'No wonder,' said Aunt Carol. 'How long's he been there?'

'Eighteen years. He went there straight from school.'

'It's a heck of a time to work at the same place. All his mates work there, don't they?'

Cheryl's mother nodded. 'That's right. They drink together, play footy together, everything. Don't get me wrong, I know how important it is to him. I just wish he didn't act as if it was the end of the world, that's all. Anyway, I'll give you a ring tomorrow, Carol.'

'OK,' said Aunt Carol. 'See you, Pat. See you, Cheryl.'

As they left, Cheryl noticed Kevin through the window in the back door. He was sitting with his back against the garden shed, stroking Domino. He was in a world of his own. Cheryl shuddered. When she saw him handling the little animal so gently, it was impossible to believe what he'd done. But that keen, handsome face hid as much as it revealed. There were demons in there.

Even then, Cheryl's turbulent day wasn't over. This time it had nothing to do with Kevin, though. It was Dad.

'Oh no,' Mum groaned the moment she set eyes on him. 'Now what? You've got a face like a smacked behind.'

'You may well ask,' her father snarled, shoving a plate of uneaten beans on toast across the kitchen table. 'It's them, my so-called mates.'

'What have they done?'

'It's what they haven't done.'

—— 42 ——

Mum sighed. 'I do hope you're going to get to the point.'

'We had another meeting,' Dad explained. 'Ever since the redundancies were announced there have been all sorts of moans and grumbles, so we got everyone together. Well, I stood up and said we ought to do something; march, write letters, go on strike, anything.'

'And you were on your own.'

Dad nodded. 'As good as. Sixteen of us out of two hundred. They were all crying out for their redundancy money. I ask you, they actually wanted to go. How stupid can you get? We can't all open a little shop or get a stall on Paddy's market. A couple of years and the cash will be gone, then what do we do?' He stabbed at the beans on toast. 'We'll be living on stuff like this. There's no work round here for labourers.'

Cheryl saw her mother rest a comforting hand on his shoulder. Dad was sitting hunched, his head bowed. He was hugging himself and his toes were turned inwards almost like a little boy's. She'd never seen him look so tired and defeated. It was scary. What are you supposed to do when one of the strongest people in your life just crumples in front of your eyes?

'I'm scared, love. I've got no trade. I mean, I've never been out of work. How will we live? What are we going to do?'

'We'll manage, Dave,' Mum answered. 'I've still got my job. The mortgage isn't much now and the car's paid off. It won't be easy, but we'll get by.'

'Get by! Not much for eighteen years' work, is it? I don't want to get by. I want to give my family a decent life. I thought maybe next year we would have enough to go to Disneyworld. I've always wanted to take the pair of you there. That's gone up in smoke, hasn't it? I've even started worrying about how much we're spending on our Cheryl's birthday.'

Mum gave a start, as if she'd only just realised Cheryl was still in the room.

'Don't start feeling sorry for yourself, Dave Tasker. You're not the first fellow to get finished up. It's even happened to me. I was made redundant from my first job in the packing factory, remember.'

'It isn't the same for a woman.'

Cheryl could almost hear the crash as Dad dropped his clanger.

'Oh, isn't it?' Mum was incensed. 'So my work doesn't count, I suppose?'

'I didn't mean—'

'And try telling our Carol it isn't the same for a woman. Three years she's been without two pennies to rub together. She'd give her right arm for a job. She'd love her kids to have the same as our Cheryl.'

Dad bridled. 'Then she shouldn't have married a villain like Tony McGovern, should she?'

Cheryl winced. Her mother's face had gone white with anger.

'Typical of a man to say that! I suppose you have to serve a life sentence for falling in love with the wrong man.'

Cheryl shrank back against the wall, her parents' words echoing inside her head. What were they doing? They never quarrelled as badly as this. She knew they must have had rows, but they'd always hidden them from her.

'She knew what he was like,' her father retorted. 'The whole family are rotten right through. Now Kev's going the same way.'

'And you've never made a mistake, have you, Mr High and Mighty Tasker!'

Cheryl's head was bursting. Like a swelling tide, it was coming her way, the end of her safe, settled life. Three years ago, when his dad walked out, all this had happened to Kev. His life had just crashed. Now the same thing seemed to be happening to her. She wanted to scream, just like she had in the park, to stop the madness, but she couldn't. There, it had been easy to see sense, but her parents' fury paralysed her. She was scared and angry, but she had no tears, no strength to shout, just the need to break away and get out of that room with its hard, clashing voices. Without a word, she turned on her heel and walked out. For a while she hovered in the kitchen, then, sick of the raised voices from the living room, she trailed aimlessly into the garden.

It was a damp, cold evening and the wintry wind was snapping fiercely at the privet hedge that separated their garden from the railway embankment. A train thundered by, slowing to enter the local station. Its lights flashed through the gloom. She smiled sadly. She loved the trains that rumbled down the line. They were the first sound in the morning and the last sound at night, the North and South of her life. So regular, so reliable.

'On its way to Ormskirk,' she said out loud.

'Wish you were on it?'

'Dad!'

Now this was a turn-up for the book. It was Mum who handled the heart-to-hearts, Dad usually retreated to his armchair until things were sorted.

'I'm sorry you had to hear that.'

'It doesn't matter,' said Cheryl, choking back her real feelings.

'It does, you know.'

Cheryl was teasing her hair.

'It was my fault,' said Dad.

—— 45 ——

'Yes,' said Cheryl. 'I know it was.'

Tossing his head back, her father gave a loud guffaw. 'Nothing like being blunt, is there?'

Cheryl was in no mood to humour him. 'You scared me,' she said.

'Sorry, love. It's all this palaver over work. It's getting me down.'

'Will things really be that bad?'

Her father ran a hand wearily over his face. 'To be honest, girl, I'm just not sure. It's hard to see how I'll get another job in a hurry, especially after today.'

'What do you mean?'

'Who's going to take on somebody who shouts his mouth off like I did? I've stuck my neck out once too often.'

'You only did what you thought was right.'

'Yes, and I'll still end up on the dole. Employers don't like people who start shouting for strikes.'

Cheryl was thoughtful for a moment. 'I just keep thinking about Kevin.'

'Kev, why?'

'His dad was out of work … when things went wrong.'

It only took her father a few moments to latch on to her wavelength. 'And you think I'd clear off and leave you? Give me some credit.'

Cheryl heard the railway line buzzing. 'Here's one going into Liverpool,' she remarked.

Her father watched it pass before speaking again. 'Between the likes of Tony McGovern and me, there's a gulf a mile wide. I'll give you a promise right now,' he said. 'Come what may, I'm not going anywhere.'

Nine

'IS SOMETHING WRONG?' ASKED HELEN.

'You could say that.'

They walked up the path from Cheryl's front door.

'Well, are you going to tell me, or is this another secret?'

Three days had gone by since Mum and Dad's row, but it was rumbling on in fits and starts. They would snap over the slightest things. That morning it had been the car. An indicator bulb had gone and Dad had ranted on about it for a good half an hour. As if some evil spirit was doing all this, toying with him. That was it, a stupid indicator bulb that would cost buttons and he droned on and on about *his luck* and how nothing ever went right for long, and how they wouldn't be able to replace anything once he was out of work. Talk about over the top!

'Mum threw a dish at my dad,' said Cheryl.

'You're kidding.'

'No, she threw it, all right.'

'Did it hurt him?'

'Oh, it wasn't meant to. She aimed for the cupboard. Gave the cat a fright, though. I think she just wanted him to shut up.' She explained about the indicator bulb.

'Does he usually get that excited about things?'

They turned left at the top of the road and stood at the pelican crossing on the main road.

'No. Mum reckons it's all the worry at work.'

'Oh.'

'Either of your parents ever lost their jobs?'

'I don't think so.'

'Don't you know?'

Helen shrugged. 'So long as I get what I want for Christmas, I'm not bothered.' Cheryl shook her head. Sometimes Helen could be as shallow as the milk at the end of your breakfast cereal. Like when it came to inviting your best friend's cousin to tea without telling her.

'Helen,' she remarked. 'You crack me up. You really do.'

They had just started to cross when a familiar figure appeared on the road which led to the Diamond.

'There's Kev,' said Helen. Her voice was all sparky with excitement. As usual.

'Yes.'

Cheryl's reply was as non-committal as she could manage.

'Do you know something?' Helen said. 'I just worked it out. Kev's only been in school ten days.'

'So what?'

'Just think about it. Things haven't half changed. Kev's changed them.'

'Yeah, maybe.'

'So are we going to wait for him?'

'No, he'll catch up if he wants to.'

'I think you're dead mean,' said Helen. '*I'm* going to wait for him.'

'Suit yourself,' said Cheryl, marching away.

'Have you two fallen out?' Helen called after her.

Cheryl's eyes were stinging and there was a lump in her throat. 'No,' she said. But she was lying.

Even in PE Helen didn't give up.

'I'll get it out of you sometime.'

Cheryl was on the rack. 'Oh, give it a rest, Helen,' she said. 'Why didn't you ask Kev, seeing as you're so pally?'

'I daren't. Those eyes go through you like a laser.'

'Well, if you daren't ask him, don't expect to get anything out of me.'

'Some friend you are. I'm dying to know.'

'I've told you. There was no row, and there's no big secret.'

They were lolling on the climbing frame, watching Kevin. He could scale the ropes like a monkey with a fire under him.

'Cheryl, Helen,' came Jacko's voice. 'Put some life into it, will you? PE is a lesson just like any other. It isn't an excuse to have a good chinwag.'

Cheryl lowered herself slowly so that she was swinging by the backs of her knees, her long hair trailing on the floor.

A moment later Helen did likewise. 'I still think my best mate ought to tell.'

Cheryl's reply was a low growl of irritation.

'And rest,' said Jacko. 'Kevin, that means you, too.'

Kevin and Jacko hadn't really hit it off. In fact, during the previous afternoon's science lesson

Kev's antics had got Jacko so wound up that he'd snapped. A pain in the neck is what he called Kevin out loud, but Helen swore he'd said something stronger under his breath. Kevin wasn't doing anything to endear himself this time, either. He lowered himself down the rope until he was just above the floor, then hung for a second, grinning mischievously.

Which was something else Jacko had said during science: 'I don't like your face.' That had had the whole class in hysterics – but at Jacko's expense. It was worth at least five bonus points to get a teacher so uptight he came out with something as naff as that.

'I said,' Jacko fumed. 'Get down.'

Curling his legs above his head, Kevin dismounted with an impromptu somersault.

'Yes, yes, very impressive,' remarked Jacko sourly.

'I thought so,' Kevin answered chirpily, earning himself some appreciative giggles.

Jacko gave him a level stare. 'Don't be so insolent, lad.'

Cheryl winced. Kevin might be cock of the school with the kids, but how he loved to provoke Jacko! He'd taken over from Jamie Moore as the class's number one wind-up merchant. No, more than taken over. He'd cornered the entire market in teacher-baiting. It was a few seconds before Jacko removed the evil eye from Kevin and was ready to continue.

'Now,' he said. 'If we're *all* quite ready.' He gave Kevin a glacial stare. 'We'll walk back to the classroom. And I do mean walk. If I catch anyone running, they can spend part of their dinner hour doing lines. Got that, Y6J?'

Judging by the nods, Y6J had got that. With a final glance in Kevin's direction, Jacko set off down the corridor. At the far end, by the dinner hall, he stopped to let Mr Hughes' class Y6H past on their way to the next PE lesson. It was a subdued Andy Ramage who drew alongside Kevin and Jamie Moore.

'Hello,' said Kevin, in his most sarcastic tone of voice. 'Look at Brain Damage, Jamie. Whatever could that be dripping down his ear?'

Andy reddened visibly.

'Do you know what?' Jamie responded, catching on quickly, 'I do believe it's custard.'

'What's up, Brain Damage,' Kevin taunted. 'Treasure

it so much you haven't washed? You must have enjoyed our little ceremony.'

Andy said something under his breath.

'What was that?' Kevin demanded. 'Did you say something to me?' The smirk had vanished from his face, and he was moving threateningly towards Andy.

'McGovern!' Jacko shouted. 'Get back into line.'

Kevin gave Andy a long, hard look, then shuffled reluctantly back into line while Mr Hughes' class continued down the corridor.

'Knock it off, will you, Kev,' said Cheryl. 'You're going to get yourself into trouble. You've proved your point. Can't you just leave him alone?'

'Cheryl,' Kevin told her, 'When I need your advice, I'll ask for it.'

'Isn't he a pain?' she groaned to Helen.

'A bit,' said Helen. 'But he's cute with it.'

Cheryl gave a long-suffering shake of the head. She tried to tell herself otherwise, but she was feeling really jealous. Not satisfied with turning her life upside down, Kevin was taking her best friend away from her.

'Hurry up and get changed,' Jacko raised his voice above the hubbub. 'Spelling test before dinner.'

There was a chorus of groans.

'And I don't want to hear that again,' snapped Jacko. Kevin's arrival at Cropper Lane clearly wasn't doing anything for his blood pressure. Until just under a fortnight before, Cheryl had always wanted to be a teacher when she grew up. Now she was re-thinking her career options – steeplejack or lion-tamer might be better, especially if you had a Kevin McGovern in your class!

Once everyone had changed and hung up their PE bags, the class was ready for their test.

'Last one,' Jacko announced. 'Architect.'

There was a rustle of conversation, before Jacko raised his hands, palms showing. It was his call-to-order signal. 'Quiet,' he ordered. 'Now, swop your spelling books and mark your neighbour's work. No, Kevin, I don't want you swopping with Jamie.'

'Why not?'

'Because.'

'But—'

'But nothing.'

'But—'

Jacko slapped his book down on the desk. 'Don't but me, son.'

Kevin gave Jamie and Helen a knowing look, 'I'm not a goat, you know.'

The usual giggles. Jacko was losing it, all right.

'Enough of your lip, McGovern. Now give your book to Helen.'

As Jacko turned his back, Kevin gave a triumphant grin. Cheryl soon discovered why. The moment Jacko started writing up the correct spellings, the pair swopped their books back.

'That's cheating,' Cheryl hissed.

'So what?' Kevin replied, a little too loudly.

'Who's talking?' Jacko demanded. 'There are talking activities and silent activities, and this one is silent. Right, check off your neighbour's answers against the spellings on the board.'

He wrote up the first spelling.

'Yes!' said Kevin.

'Sh,' ordered Jacko, before writing up the second spelling.

'Yes,' Kevin announced again.

Jacko spun round. 'I don't want to hear that stupid noise again. Got that?'

He wrote up the third spelling. With a knowing smirk

in the direction of Helen and Jamie, Kevin did it again.
'Yes!'

'Who *was* that?' Jacko demanded. 'I said: who was that?'

But nobody was about to split on Kevin.

'Well, it's the last time,' said Jacko.

He was wrong. No sooner had he written the next spelling up than the loud, mocking 'Yes' was heard again. Jacko slammed down the chalk, crushing it into dust.

'It was you, McGovern.'

You could tell when Jacko was annoyed. Christian names went right out of the window.

'What?'

'You heard. You're the one who made that stupid noise.'

'I never!'

'Don't talk back, lad.'

'But I never did it. You're wrong.'

Jacko stormed over to his desk. 'You're on a warning, McGovern.' Then, spitting fury over Kevin's cheek, the words came out in a boiling cascade: '*Andifyousomuchas-lookthewrongwayoncemoreinthislessonI'llhaveyou—Got-that!*'

Breathless, Jacko chalked *KM* on the board then strode down the aisle between the desks in Kevin's direction. And that's when he spotted Kevin's spelling book.

'What's this? You've been changing the answers.' He picked up the book. 'And I thought I told you to swop with Helen. You've been cheating.'

'No, I haven't.'

Kevin was set on confrontation. He was cool with it, much cooler than Jacko, who'd lost his temper completely. His face was red and sweaty, and his eyes were bulging. On his day, Kevin knew how to rattle a teacher, all right.

'That's it,' bawled Jacko. 'Out! Go and stand outside the door. I'll deal with you later.'

It was a few moments before he had recovered his composure sufficiently to continue with the spellings. When the bell finally went, he dismissed the class and called Kevin back inside.

'Lines, you reckon?' asked Helen.

'Probably,' Cheryl answered wearily. 'That's if Jacko doesn't send him to Mrs Harrison.'

'He loves to get Jacko going, doesn't he?'

'Yes, he's really stupid. Anyway, forget about our Kev, are you still coming to my birthday party?'

'Of course I am,' said Helen, before turning back to watch Kevin and Jacko through the classroom window. 'Will Kev be there?'

Cheryl managed to hide her impatience at Helen's question. 'Sure, he's my cousin, isn't he?'

'Then,' Helen told her, 'I'm definitely coming.' She pointed at Kevin taking a sheet of paper off Jacko. 'I told you he'd get lines. Why do you think he does it?'

Cheryl sighed. 'I only wish I knew.'

She did know, of course, but she still wasn't telling.

Ten

FUNNY, ISN'T IT, DAD? YOU HAVE THESE WISHES, BUT the moment they come true they're never enough When I started at Cropper Lane, what did I want? To fit in, to make some new friends, to forget about the old estate. Well, I've done all that and more. Take Brain Damage. I bet he wishes he'd never heard of Kevin McGovern. I'm the Guv'nor, his worst nightmare.

It isn't enough, though. Inside of me, there's this fire burning. I can't seem to leave it alone. I mean, Mum would die if she knew what I was doing. She'd just die. Like today. I just had to have another go at Brain Damage. Sometimes I wonder myself what makes me do it. It's like something's driving me, like I've got to take on the whole world and win single-handed. Cheryl says it's because I want to pick on somebody worse off than me. What does she know? She's a girl, for crying out loud. She's always got her hand up, trying to please Jacko. I ask you, who wants to be a suck? He kept me in today. As if that'll make me toe the line! I really hate teachers – and social workers. They all think they can tell me what to do. Well, they can't. If they knew half of what me and Rooster used to get up to on the old estate, their hair would turn white.

You want to know what makes me tick? I'll tell you. I'm fighting a war. It's like the world's saying: 'Be like everybody else. Do as you're told.' And I'm fighting back, telling them I am somebody, I'm the Guv'nor. I don't want to be another little clockwork kid with a key sticking out of his back, doing just what he's told all the time. I bet you understand. Do you know that they still talk about you on the old estate, Dad? Three years you've been gone and I still kept hearing about you down there. You'd never win a popularity contest, but you definitely made your mark.

That's what I want to do; I want to take the world by the scruff of the neck and shake it until it begs for mercy. I'm going to make it do exactly what I want.

I'm going to make my mark.

Eleven

'HI THERE, GARETH,' SAID CHERYL.
Her little cousin was standing on the doorstep, holding out a parcel in one hand and clutching a half-licked Tangle-Twister in the other.

'Is this for me?'

'It's a T-shirt,' said Gareth. 'Save the elephants.' Only he pronounced it elm-phlants.

'Gareth,' Aunt Carol chided. 'You've spoilt the surprise. You're meant to let Cheryl find out for herself.'

'That's all right, Aunty Carol,' said Cheryl. 'I don't mind.'

'Where's Kevin?' asked Helen.

'Good question,' said Aunt Carol, stepping back on to the garden path. 'Kevin, get a move on.'

Kevin was trudging along the street, scuffing his trainers on the pavement.

'What's up with him now?' asked Cheryl.

'Ignore grizzleguts,' said Aunt Carol. 'He's in a big nark because I had a go at him. Mr Jackson called me in over his behaviour this afternoon. Didn't you know?'

'No.'

'Anyway, I chewed the ears off him over it.'

'Oh.'

'"Oh" is right. I can't wait to get through a whole day without him causing me heartache. You're a good boy, though, aren't you, Gareth?'

Gareth smiled a red and green lolly-ice smile. Cheryl smiled too. Angels with dirty faces.

'Hi there, Kev,' said Helen. At least *she* was glad to see him.

'Hello.'

'Anyway,' said Cheryl, dismissing Kevin's glum reply. 'Let's get on with the party.'

The party was Helen, Cheryl, Kevin and half a dozen schoolfriends, Gareth and another younger cousin. They played pass the parcel for the younger children's benefit before tucking into the buffet.

'Is your dad coming?' asked Helen through a mouthful of sausage roll.

'He's still down South,' said Kevin, before beating a hasty retreat.

Gareth gave a puzzled look. His mouth, now caked in layers of lolly ice, cheese spread and crisps opened in protest. 'But—'

Kevin hissed something in his ear.

'Mum.' wailed Gareth. 'Kevin said a naughty word.'

'Did you?' Aunt Carol demanded.

'No,' Kevin pouted. 'He's lying.'

'I am not,' Gareth yelled. 'He said the g-word.'

Suddenly everybody was mouthing the same question around the kitchen. 'What's rude and starts with g?'

'Gareth love,' his mother said with a smile. 'I don't think there *are* any naughty words starting with a g.'

Cheryl felt sorry for her little cousin. He just didn't understand why everybody was laughing.

'Funny, isn't it?' Helen mused thoughtfully. 'Every time I mention his dad, Kevin changes the subject.'

Cheryl was determined not to be drawn.

'There is no dad, is there?' Helen asked doggedly.

'Oh, there's a dad, all right,' Cheryl replied.

'Is that the big secret, then?' Helen asked. 'Something his dad's done?'

'Don't be daft.'

'Then what?'

'You know I'm not going to tell. Why won't you just let it drop?'

At that moment her mother came to the rescue. 'Have you all had enough savouries?' she asked. 'Right, time for the birthday cake.'

Everybody clustered round the table.

'Can I light the candles?' Kevin asked, picking up a box of matches from the kitchen table.

'You!' his mother blazed, snatching the box off him. Don't even think about it.' Her eyes were flashing and her face set in a deep, threatening frown.

Cheryl glimpsed the surprised look on her friends' faces.

Aunt Carol gave Kevin a withering glare, then opened the matches. 'I'll do it,' she said. 'Turn the lights out.'

Cheryl's mum nodded and plunged the room into darkness, lit first by one then eventually by all eleven candles.

'Come on now, Cheryl. Make a wish and blow them out in one go.'

Cheryl looked at the flickering candles. By their light she could see Helen watching Kevin keenly. Now her mind really was working overtime. Cheryl took a deep breath and blew the candles out, but as soon as she sat back in her chair they re-lit.

'Trick candles!' Gareth squealed delightedly. 'Look, Kev, they're boss.' He'd obviously forgiven his big brother the whispered threat, even if he did use the g-word.

Eventually the trick candles were replaced by real ones and Cheryl succeeded in blowing them out. While everyone sang 'Happy Birthday', Helen's eyes remained fixed firmly on Kevin. There was only one thing for it; Cheryl would have to avoid her until she could think of a plausible explanation.

As it turned out, it wasn't much of a plan. Helen's dad wasn't coming for her until after nine o'clock and she would be the last to leave.

Sod's law.

'I'll help you clear up,' Cheryl told her mother, as the last guest left and Helen made a bee-line towards her.

'No need,' said her mother. 'It is your birthday. Why don't you and Helen occupy yourselves until her father arrives?'

That, thought Cheryl, is the last thing I need.

'Well,' said Helen, as they settled in front of Cheryl's new pop-video. '*Now* are you going to tell me?'

There was a wrenching feeling in Cheryl's stomach. 'I can't.'

'What was all that fuss over the matches?' Helen asked. 'Has that got something to do with it?'

Cheryl's insides were twisting like a corkscrew. 'Give over, will you?'

'I'll find out,' said Helen. 'Like I found out about your Uncle Tony.'

Cheryl gaped.

'You didn't think it would take me long, did you?' she asked.

'But how …?'

'How do you think? I asked Kev's mum.'

'You never!'

'Of course I did. I came right out with it. I just asked if Kev's dad was coming to the party, so she explained. Dead easy, really. I think she wanted to talk about it. She told me everything.'

—— 60 ——

Cheryl squinted doubtfully at her friend. She was bluffing, she had to be.

'I know he cleared off three years ago,' Helen continued, dispelling Cheryl's ideas about a bluff. 'I know he was a boxer. And ...' Helen paused for effect. 'I know he was a bit of a scally.'

'Did Aunt Carol say that?'

'She didn't have to. It's the way she spoke about him, you know, like she was a bit ashamed. Anyway, you've just confirmed it.'

Cheryl realized she'd been conned. 'That was a mean trick, Helen,' she protested.

'Not half as mean as keeping the secret to yourself,' Helen retorted. 'Oh, come on, Cheryl. It can't be half as bad as you make out.'

'Helen, you can't even begin to imagine.'

Stupid, Cheryl snapped at herself. What did I say that for?

'Oh,' Helen groaned in exasperation, 'I'll burst if you don't tell me. I'll just burst.'

'Well, don't make a mess on the wallpaper,' said Cheryl. 'Because I'm not telling.'

There was a knock at the front door, followed by Mum's voice. 'It's your dad, Helen.'

'You wriggled out of it this time,' said Helen. 'But I'll find out. You see if I don't.'

Twelve

CHERYL KNEW TROUBLE WAS BREWING THE moment she walked into the yard the following morning. A dozen kids were crowded round the back of the boiler house.

'What is it?' she asked apprehensively.

'The bins,' Jamie told her. 'Somebody set light to them last night. Mrs Harrison's on the warpath.'

Cheryl stared disbelievingly at the huge, black scorch-mark on the breeze-block wall of the boiler house. No wonder the head was blazing.

'Have they caught anybody?'

'I don't think so,' Jamie answered. 'But they will.'

'What makes you say that?'

'I heard her talking to Hush Puppy.'

Hush Puppy was the school caretaker. On account of his shoes, most said, a pair of greasy, balding suedes. Or his droopy eyes and sagging jowls. Cheryl thought it might be because he was barking mad.

'What did she say?'

'That she had a good idea who'd done it.'

'She said that!'

'Yes. Why, what's eating you?'

Cheryl shook her head. It couldn't be.

'Hey Guv,' shouted Jamie suddenly. 'Seen this?'

At the announcement of her cousin's arrival, Cheryl

turned. Helen was with him. So that was why she hadn't been on the corner as usual.

'What is it?' Kevin asked, his eyes flicking questioningly in Cheryl's direction.

'Just look, will you?' said Jamie. 'Somebody's tried to burn the school down.'

Kevin's eyes fixed Cheryl. She could read the message in them: What do you think you're looking at?

'There are some mad beggars around, aren't there, Kev?' Jamie said.

'Yes,' Kevin answered, glaring pointedly at Cheryl. 'Mad.'

Those piercing, dark eyes only made the blister of doubt more painful.

'Imagine,' said Helen. 'Trying to burn the school down!' She sounded appalled, but only that she hadn't been the first to break the news. 'So when did it happen?'

'Last night,' said a gruff voice. It was Hush Puppy. 'It'll be them lads from the Comp. I'll lay any money on it. Mrs Harrison reckons she knows who did it. I bet I could give her a couple of names from last year's Y6. There were some rum 'uns in that lot, I can tell you.'

'You never know,' said Helen. 'It could be somebody who's still here.'

'What makes you say that?' Cheryl snapped.

'Just a thought,' Helen replied. 'What are you getting your knickers in a twist about?'

Cheryl bit her lip. She was all too aware of Helen's inquisitive eyes on her.

'Anyway,' said Hush Puppy, 'Off you go, kids. I've got to clean this lot up. Look, Mrs Harrison's going to blow the whistle.'

'Mrs Harrison!' Cheryl's heart missed a beat. 'Since when did she blow the whistle? She *must* be on the warpath.'

The lines were usually a disorderly throng of wrestling, shouting kids defying the teachers' best efforts to settle them down. Not this morning. Under the watchful gaze of the head, they lined up almost quietly. Curiosity about the fire ensured their complete attention.

'Good morning, children,' she began.

'Good morning, Mrs Harrison,' they chorussed.

'Most of you have probably heard about the incident which occurred sometime last night. Somebody set fire to the wheelie bins at the back of the boiler house. Luckily, the fire didn't spread. The police have been informed. I have to stress that arson is a serious offence. If anyone knows anything, anything at all, it will be treated in the utmost confidence.'

Jamie looked confused. 'What?'

'What's up, thicko?' asked Helen. 'Do I have to translate for you? It's simple. If somebody spills their guts, Mrs Harrison won't give their name away.'

'Oh.'

Cheryl glanced behind at Kevin. He couldn't have. Not at his own school.

'Thank you, staff,' said Mrs Harrison, addressing the teachers. 'You may take your classes in now.'

Cheryl hung up her bag and slid into her seat. She was all jittery, like Dad when Everton were 1–0 down with five minutes to go. She was dying to talk to Kevin, to remove the doubt that was eating away at her like acid.

'OK, Y6J,' said Jacko, clearing his voice. 'We'll take the register.'

He read down the list. 'Tracey Jarman.'

'Yes, Mr Jackson.'

'Mark Jones.'

'Good morning to you, Mr Jackson.'

'Creep,' hissed Helen.

'Kevin McGovern.' Then the flustered correction. 'Oh, office.'

Cheryl's head whipped round. It was true. He wasn't in his seat. There was only one explanation. Mrs Harrison must have collared him on the way in from the yard. The doubt that had been smouldering began to lick fiercely round her heart.

'Oh, Kev.'

'What did you say?' Helen asked.

'Nothing.'

'Danny Stone,' Jacko continued.

'Yes.' But it came out as a sullen Yuh.

Danny was another of the group of boys who together constituted Jacko's bed of nails.

'Yes what?'

'Yes, Mr Jackson.' Make that: Yuh, Midder Jackuhn.

At that point, while Jacko was considering whether to make an issue of it, the door creaked open and Kevin came in.

'Sit yourself down, Kevin,' Jacko instructed quietly before turning back to the register.

Cheryl watched Kevin's uncomfortable walk to his place. Gone was his usual swagger. Curious eyes were following him.

'Cheryl Tasker.'

She heard the words, but they were hollow, stripped of meaning. It wasn't her name she heard, more a dull, incoherent mumble.

'Cheryl, are you with us?'

A ripple of laughter alerted her.

'Oh, sorry, Mr Jackson. Here.'

'Thank you,' said Jacko. 'Some of us seem to have left our brains in bed this morning.'

Having marked Gary Young absent, Jacko closed the

register. 'Right class, let's take another look at direct speech.'

Amid the groans, Helen leaned across. 'Where do you think Kevin's been?'

Cheryl just stared ahead.

If she'd so much as ventured a reply, she would have burst into tears.

'Hey, I want a word with you.'

Cheryl felt the sharp tug on her sleeve, and the sensation of being spun round by a strong hand.

'Where's Miss Blabbermouth got to?' Kevin demanded.

'That's no way to talk about your new girlfriend,' sniped Cheryl.

'Girlfriend, my foot,' said Kevin. 'I didn't ask her to wait for me. So where is she?'

'Taking a message to the office,' Cheryl answered, encouraged to hear Kevin wasn't too keen on Helen's crush on him.

'Good.'

He drew her over to the railings, out of the hearing of the rest of their classmates.

'So what do you think you were playing at this morning?'

'I don't know what you mean.'

'Yes, you do. You thought it was me, didn't you?'

Admitting it would amount to betrayal. And she was in the salvation game.

'Get lost.'

'I saw the way you looked at me. Why didn't you just come out and accuse me?'

'Stop it,' said Cheryl hotly. 'Of course I didn't think it was you.'

'I bet you didn't! I know you've got it in for me.'

'Are you stupid?' cried Cheryl. 'Don't you know I'm trying to help you?'

'Help me? You!'

'Yes, me.'

'You're the one who needs help.'

Cheryl took a deep breath. The Good Samaritan never had it this hard! 'So what did Mrs Harrison want?'

'Not what you think,' Kevin said irritably.

'But what *did* she want?'

'To talk about the fire.'

Cheryl frowned.

'The neighbours saw who did it,' Kevin explained. 'They gave the police their descriptions. Three lads about fifteen. So I'm out of the frame.'

'Then why …?'

'Mrs Harrison wanted to reassure me I wasn't under suspicion. She's got all my reports from the old school, so she knows my history. My move up here was a bit like a free transfer. Ma Harrison had to agree to have me. Do you know what? She said she'd got faith in me. Stupid old bat.'

'But that's good.'

'You reckon?'

'Of course I do.'

'Well, I don't. How come everybody's so interested in me all of a sudden? Nobody gave a tuppenny damn before I set the fire that time.'

'Yes they did.'

'Like who?'

'Like everybody. Me, your mum …'

'Yes? So why do you jump to conclusions every time something happens? Trust me, do you? Tell it to the marines.'

With that, Kevin strode away. Cheryl shook her head. Poor Kevin, always so angry with the world. She turned to look for Helen, but to her horror her friend had already found her. She was leaning against the old bike sheds, no more than a couple of strides away.

'How long have you been there?' asked Cheryl, her neck prickling.

'Long enough,' said Helen. 'Long enough.'

Thirteen

TYPICAL, ISN'T IT? OH YES, THEY ALL TRUST ME. UNTIL something happens. Sometimes I feel as if I spend my time walking on razor blades. Nobody ever does me any favours. Look at Ma Harrison. Why did she have to drag me out of the line like that? A good way of getting everybody talking, that was. Why didn't she just write it up on the blackboard – Kev McGovern lights fires.

Mind you, it's Cheryl who annoyed me most. Even she thought I must have done it. Trust? Pull the other one, it's got a brass band on the end! Sure, I'm no angel. I never claimed to be, but why won't anybody ever give me a chance? Wipe the slate clean, they said. Make a new start, they said. That's right, that's what they said; the copper who cautioned me, the social worker, my mum, everybody. It's a funny sort of trust when they spend all their time watching me like I'm some sort of public health hazard. I can just imagine it: 'Bad case of the Kevins, Mrs McGovern. I advise rat poison.'

I'll tell you one thing, Dad, you're better off out of all this, wherever you are. You never really get a second chance, do you? I'm sick of the lot of them. If they want me to go back to my old ways, they're going the right way about it.

Fourteen

'OK, YOU'VE PUT ME OFF LONG ENOUGH. NOW cough.'

Long enough! No, nowhere near long enough. Kev had hardly been in school a fortnight and the lid was already being prised off his secret. Cheryl leaned back and stared up at the darkening sky. There was a smell of burning in the air. Somebody had lit their bonfire early. She crossed her arms, as if trying to hug her body warmth to her. There in the garden, it was bitterly cold.

'I wish you'd never overheard us,' she said.

'Well, I did, so let's have it.'

Cheryl had been trying to keep Helen at arm's length ever since the morning break. She tried wishing the whole thing away. If only she could be a little girl again. She'd been wishing all day that she was, then Mum could kiss the hurt away and everything would be all right again. The trouble is, she wasn't little any more and she was realizing that her parents couldn't make everything all right any more. They had problems of their own. Cheryl had to face this one alone, she knew that. And yet her heart still ached for it to be all a bad dream. She wanted to lose that day and start all over again, but time's not like an alarm clock. It can't be turned back when it goes wrong. In the end, only a promise to tell all had satisfied her friend. Now, the reckoning had come.

'Well?' Helen demanded.

Cheryl knew she didn't owe Helen anything. She could still clam up. Yes, that was the right thing to do. And yet ... There was this great need to be free of the secret. It filled her until she felt she would burst.

'You know part of it already,' said Cheryl, uneasily aware of her mother standing at the lighted kitchen window, washing the dishes. 'It's fire.'

'Go on.'

Cheryl glanced again at her mother just the other side of the kitchen window. This was wrong. There was still time to stop. But she wasn't going to stop.

'It might cure you of the stupid crush you've got on him,' she said spitefully.

'That's for me to say,' said Helen.

Cheryl hated herself for what she had said, but she still didn't stop. She wasn't like Kevin. She didn't have his strength.

'Promise you won't tell a living soul,' she said. 'Not even your mum.'

'I already have promised.'

'Promise!'

'OK, OK, I promise. Cross my heart and hope to die.'

Cheryl felt as if she were walking off the edge of a cliff. Deep down, she knew the promise was meaningless. Even as she began to tell the story, she had a terrible feeling, as if she were tumbling into darkness, a darkness deeper and more complete than anything she had ever known. But she had taken the step, and there was no clawing her way back. 'It happened on the estate where Kevin used to live, down in Kirkdale.'

Helen nodded, pressing her to continue.

'Kevin started knocking round with this bunch of lads. I played out with them a couple of times when we were visiting, but I can't say I liked them very much. There was one in particular, Rooster.'

'Rooster!'

'His real name's Albert Lugmore.'

'No wonder he prefers Rooster!'

Cheryl was curling and un-curling her hair. 'Anyway, Rooster's trouble. He used to dare Kevin to walk along the wall at Kirkdale station.'

This is wrong, wrong! she cried inside. 'I can't say any more.'

'Oh, but you're going to,' Helen told her. 'There's no backing out now.'

'But Helen—'

'But Helen nothing. Now cough.'

'I shouldn't.'

Helen gave her a long stare. 'So did Kev do it?'

'What?'

'Walk along the wall.'

There was no going back. Cheryl felt so weary, but she went on with the story. 'Of course he did. Anyway, like I said, Rooster gets up to all sorts. He tried to get me to smoke. Then they started to mess about with matches. It was a laugh most of the time, but Kevin was fascinated by fire. He would set light to crisp packets and watch them crinkling up. He's a bit weird about it.'

'And that's it?' asked Helen. 'He's got a thing about crisp packets?'

'Of course that isn't it!' groaned Cheryl. Was this the friend she expected to keep the secret? 'Are you going to listen, or not?'

'I'm listening.'

'Rooster used to egg Kevin on. That's the type he is, sly, always trying to get other people into trouble, even his mates.'

'Nice lad!'

'My mum got a phone call one night. It was Aunt

Carol. She was in a dreadful state. It turned out Kevin and Rooster had lit a fire in this pensioner's garden—'

'You're joking!'

Cheryl ignored the rather unconvincing exclamation of horror. Helen was excited, completely hooked on the story. Cheryl recognized the feeling. Normally, she too would have been fascinated. But that was when the events took place over there somewhere, to other people. Not when it was your own flesh and blood.

Cheryl forced out the words. 'This old bloke's pigeon cote went up in flames. Well, when Kevin and Rooster couldn't put it out, they got scared and ran off. What they didn't know was that the old fellow was mad about his birds. He was living on his own and they were his only company.'

'What happened? Did he get burned alive?'

'No, nothing like that,' Cheryl replied. 'He must have had a weak heart or something. When he saw the fire he tried to rescue his pigeons, but it was too much for him. He had a heart attack.'

Helen's eyes were as round as saucers. 'So he did die?'

'That's right,' Cheryl confirmed sadly. 'Kevin didn't mean it, but nobody saw it like that. Some of the old man's family came round making threats. One night a brick came through the window. I suppose you can understand it in a way, but it wasn't fair. The brick just missed Gareth. Aunt Carol was scared stiff. Kev didn't mean it, you see, the fire was an accident. Still, none of the neighbours would talk to them. In the end, she asked for a transfer up here.'

'No wonder she's so edgy about matches!'

'She's been really down on Kevin since then, but it just makes him worse. He's like a bomb waiting to go off. It's a real mess.'

'It sounds it.'

Cheryl turned towards her friend. She was over-whelmed with panic. She'd said it, she'd told. 'You won't mention it to anyone, will you? If it got out …'

'I told you,' Helen insisted. 'My lips are sealed.'

Cheryl just stood there, looking pleadingly at her friend, willing her to keep silent about Kevin's secret, willing her not to be the school gossip.

'But what about Kev's dad?' Helen asked. 'Where does he fit into all this?'

'Uncle Tony? He doesn't really. He's been gone years.' Cheryl didn't like being questioned about Tony McGovern. The very name was full of menace.

'Kev still talks about him, though. He makes up all sorts of stories.'

'I know he does.'

'It was obvious Kev was lying about him. All that stuff about being down South. Was he really such a villain?'

Cheryl found the intensity of Helen's curiosity threat-ening. It was a reminder of a family broken to pieces, a time when all the little rules and routines that held things together had stopped operating.

'Oh, I don't know. It's all so long ago. Haven't you got anything better to worry about?'

'To be honest,' Helen replied disarmingly. 'No.'

'Well, it's no use pumping me about Uncle Tony,' Cheryl told her morosely. 'I don't know that much more than you. It's three years since he cleared off and nobody's heard of him since.'

'Not at all? Not even at Christmas and birthdays?'

'I don't think so. Mind you, Mum and Dad wouldn't mention it even if they had.'

'Fancy having all this going on in your family,' Helen sighed. 'We're all dead boring at my house. I wish something like this was happening to us.'

A voice inside screamed: If only you knew what it's like. Helen, you fool. You fool!

'You should thank your lucky stars it isn't,' Cheryl told her grimly.

'Get away. It's fan-tastic.'

'That's all right for you to say. You don't have to live with it.'

Cheryl noticed her mother drying her hands. 'Shush. Here comes Mum.'

'How long are you going to be out there?' she called, opening the back door. 'It's getting cold.'

'We'll be in now,' said Cheryl.

As the back door closed. Cheryl seized Helen's wrist. The very idea of what she had done was driving her mad. 'You mustn't tell anyone what I've just told you. Not a soul.'

'How many more times, Cheryl? I won't say a word.'

A rocket climbed into the night sky and exploded into a shower of red flares.

'Fireworks,' said Helen. 'Somebody's early. It's not November till next week.'

'For some of us,' said Cheryl ruefully. 'It's fireworks every day.'

'How could you?'

Kevin planted himself in front of her. He was trembling, his fists clenched tightly by his sides. He was rage, all rage, diamond hard and brutish.

'Pardon.'

'You can cut that out, Cheryl,' he cried. 'You know exactly what I mean. I know it was you. It had to be.'

Cheryl shivered, but it wasn't the chilly air of the playground. The night before, as she'd opened her heart to Helen, she had been falling. Now she was about to hit the ground.

'You had to blab it all round school, didn't you? Some cousin you are.'

Her flesh tingled. Oh no, please, not this.

'But I didn't!'

'So how come Jamie's just asked me about the fire, eh? How else could he know?'

Cheryl hung her head. 'It must have been Helen. She's the only one I told.'

'Why?' Kevin's face was white with anger. 'What did you tell her for? Why did you have to tell anyone?'

Every bit of Cheryl was filled with a dull, grinding ache. 'I had to. She'd already guessed.'

'Guessed! How do you guess something like that?'

'She was in the bike sheds yesterday morning, eavesdropping.'

Judging by Kevin's furrowed brow, he still wasn't quite on her wavelength.

'When we were arguing about the fire in the bins.'

Kevin closed his eyes in a gesture of despair. 'Couldn't you have at least thought of something better than the truth? Surely you could have come up with some sort of explanation. Can you imagine what Brain Damage is going to do with this?'

'But Kev, I didn't mean it to come out.' she sobbed. 'I was angry with you ...'

'Angry? Why?'

'You and Helen. She's my best friend ...'

'And that's it! You split on me for that?'

'Helen's the only one I've told,' said Cheryl. 'And I made her promise not to tell.'

'Great,' said Kevin sarcastically. 'And she really knows how to stick to her promises, doesn't she?'

Cheryl was aware of Mark Jones and Danny Stone pointing in their direction. They obviously knew Kevin's secret.

'There he is,' Danny whispered excitedly.

'Listen to that, will you?' Kevin groaned. 'See what you've done?

'But I didn't mean it.'

'Oh, so that makes it all right, I suppose? Well, you've sunk me now. You've done me in good style. The council won't move us again. What do I do now? Just tell me that.'

Cheryl lowered her eyes. She just couldn't face him.

Kevin shook his head, and with a gesture of disgust, he walked away.

Cheryl felt suddenly alone, standing in a corner of the playground with the discarded crisp packets whipping round her legs in the wind. She pulled up her coat collar, wishing that she could hide her face from the world. How could it all have ended in such a mess? Wasn't she the one who had the grand plan, the one who was going to save Kevin? There must have been a way to keep Kevin's secret, even after Helen had overheard them. But she hadn't thought of it. She hadn't even tried. She'd only thought of herself, her spite and jealousy and most of all the need to share the secret with somebody. Despite her mission to save him, she'd simply thrown Kevin to the wolves.

A couple of Year Three boys drifted by.

'Hey Miggsy, heard the latest?'

'No, what?'

'It's Guv, the new kid.'

'Yeah, the one who bullies the bullies, I know him. So what's he done?'

'He killed somebody, burned them alive.'

'That's a load of rubbish.'

'Ask Jimbo if you don't believe me. He reckons Guv locked this fellow in his shed then set fire to it.'

'Are you winding me up?'

'No way. It's the gospel truth.'

The second boy gave a low whistle, then the pair of them ran away to play off-ground tick. It seemed as if everyone was talking about it. Heads were turning in Kevin's direction. It was the hottest news in the school ever.

Cheryl watched miserably as the rumours spread like wildfire. There was no stopping it now. Already the story of Kevin and the fire was becoming a legend. It had overtaken the truth and there seemed no way of recovering it.

'Is it true?' asked a girl in a faded anorak.

Cheryl didn't meet her eyes. 'Is what true?'

'As if you didn't know. Your cousin. Did he really kill somebody?'

'Don't be stupid, Karen.'

'Who's being stupid? I asked you if it's true.'

Cheryl's silence was enough. 'It is true!' she cried triumphantly. 'I knew it was. Imagine that, we've got a murderer in the school.'

'Kevin isn't a murderer,' Cheryl protested indignantly.

The argument had drawn a cluster of girls.

'What do you call it, then?' asked one.

'Yes, he burned somebody, didn't he? Sounds like murder to me, all right.'

'You don't know anything,' shrieked Cheryl, her face white with anger and shame.

'Shout all you like,' sneered Karen. 'We're not the ones with a killer in the family.'

As the group around her dispersed, Cheryl caught sight of Andy Ramage. He was standing with his mates, staring straight ahead. The focus of their attention wasn't difficult to discover. Just a few metres away, on his own for the first time since he had arrived at Cropper Lane, stood Kevin.

Fifteen

*C*ALL THIS LIVING? MY OWN COUSIN, MY OWN BLOOD,
*and she grasses me up. And you know why? Cheryl
was jealous. Yeah, jealous. Pathetic, isn't it? I couldn't give
a monkeys about drippy Helen. I'll tell you what, Dad,
from now on I trust nobody. Got that, nobody. It's me
against the world. I'm going to look out for number one.
You know what I feel like doing? I want to burn. I just
can't help thinking about it. Fire's part of me. A few days
ago, I was the leader of the pack, the Guv'nor. I was
somebody. I bet it's like when you won your cups and
medals boxing. I used to go and look at them in that glass
case in our living room. You know what I thought. My
dad is somebody, he matters. Even when you and Mum
had your rows, I never thought any different. I knew it
wasn't your fault. Mum just didn't understand. But I did.
I knew what made you the way you were. I knew why you
had to fight. Well, that's how I wanted to be, a hard-
knock, number one. I had a feeling I was on my way too, I
was getting there.*

*But now … You know what they're saying at school?
They reckon I burned the bloke's house down. I ask you! I
wouldn't even have hurt the birds, never mind the old
fellow. We just saw a plank missing off the fence and
sneaked through. Rooster made it a sort of dare, just like he
always does. He bet me I wouldn't make a fire in the
garden. So I did it, didn't I? I had to show I had some*

bottle. I didn't mean anything by it. I mean, that doesn't make me a murderer, does it? It could happen to anyone. I was in the wrong place at the wrong time, that's all.

One minute we were laughing, watching the flames licking round the pile of twigs, the next this shed had caught fire. I didn't even know there were any pigeons in there. So that was it, we legged it.

We never even saw the old man. How were we supposed to know he'd run in there like that?

Look at me now, Dad. Crying, blubbing my eyes out. Some hard case! What would Brain Damage think if he could see me now?

Brain Damage! I can't get his eyes out of my mind. I thought he was bound to have a go at me today, but he just stood there with his mates, eye-balling me. And smiling. All the time he was watching me, there was this sly smile on his face. I just wish he'd get on with it. Fists you can fight, but this! I just know he'll be waiting for me tomorrow, him and his mates. I'm scared, Dad, it's all falling apart and I don't know what to do. On Friday it felt like everybody was on my side. Today, I'm on my own. Nobody's coming near me, not even Jamie. Bashir hung around for a bit, but what use would he be? I just ignored him and he cleared off.

Cheryl's really done for me. I'm sunk without a trace. I've been through all this before, sent to Coventry, talked about by the whole school and everybody on the estate. I couldn't go through it again, I just couldn't. Couldn't …

And I'll tell you what. I'm not going to. No, no way are they going to put one over on me. Oh, they can think they've beat me if they like. That's what I want them to think. I'll let them have their moment. I'll grovel, lick boots if that's what it takes. Then just when they think they've won, just when they've got it in their tiny minds that the Guv'nor's dead and buried, you know what? That's when

I'll get them back. And make no mistake, the more they make me suffer, the more I'll pay them back.

That's a promise.

Sixteen

CHERYL HAD A NAME FOR IT — THE PHONEY WAR. Everybody was being cool towards Kevin, but nothing had actually happened. At least, she didn't think so. The mood he was in, Kevin wasn't about to discuss it with her. If she so much as came near, he would clear off straight away. But as far as she knew, Brain Damage had left him alone. No kicks, no thumps, nothing nasty in his desk, she couldn't understand it at all. For all that, she couldn't shift the clenching feeling in her stomach.

It was going to happen, it had to, and soon.

'Cheryl,' Jacko called, 'Would you and Kevin like to go out into the corridor and work on the computer? You can use that new programme to design a front cover for our book of firework poems.'

Cheryl nodded. Jacko wasn't daft. He knew what was going on, even if he didn't come right out with it.

'Come on, Kev,' she said. 'You heard what Mr Jackson said.'

Kevin didn't answer. He didn't even look at her. He just rose slowly from his seat, his shoulders hunched in a gesture that said; leave me alone, world, I've had enough.

'Do you want to do it?' she asked as she jiggled the Mouse round the pad.

'Suit yourself.'

Cheryl went through the motions without any enthusiasm. She felt for Kevin, but he was making it hard for her.

Every time she tried to talk to him, he simply froze her out.

'Uh oh,' she groaned as she glimpsed a reflection in the screen. 'We've got visitors.'

Andy Ramage was standing behind them, a slight smirk playing on his lips.

'What are you grinning about?' Cheryl snapped.

'Now, let me see, what could I have to smile about?' mused Andy. 'Maybe this cousin of yours could tell me.'

'Get knotted,' said Cheryl. She was astonished to hear herself saying it, but equally surprised that Kevin hadn't risen to the bait.

'Tut tut, such language,' Andy taunted. 'And you used to be such a nice girl.'

'Just take a hike, will you?'

'Don't go getting yourself upset,' Andy said. 'Anyone would think he'd got something to hide.' Cheryl placed a gently restraining hand on Kevin's arm, but it wasn't needed. He just sat there, passively taking everything Andy could throw at him. She couldn't understand it at all.

'Shouldn't you be back in class, Ramage?' she asked. 'Hughesy will be wondering what you're up to.'

Andy chuckled. 'Sorry to disappoint you, Cheryl, but it was Hughesy who sent me out here.'

She snorted. It figured, he was always being thrown out of class for bad behaviour. There were weeks when he seemed to spend half his breaks outside the Head's office. He did more lines than a phone engineer.

'Ignore him,' she advised, but Andy's taunts hadn't caused even a flicker of annoyance in Kev. He just stayed in his seat, his head slightly bowed, soaking up the punishment. Curiously, his composure gave Cheryl no pleasure. Instead, there was a cold gnaw of anxiety inside her, and nothing could ease it.

A few moments went by, with Andy's eyes fixed on the back of Kevin's neck, and Kevin's eyes concentrated equally firmly on the computer screen. In the end the tense silence was broken by Helen's voice. 'Hey, Jacko wants you back in class for a minute. He wants to give out the homework.'

Cheryl was aware of heads turning as she and Kevin walked in.

'There's no need to sit down,' said Jacko. 'I just wanted you to listen to me for a sec. I'd like everyone to take one of these folders home tonight.' He held one up. 'You've got to do the sections on pages thirteen and fourteen on symmetry. OK, that's all, pop them away in your desks till hometime and don't forget to take them. Cheryl and Kevin, you can go back on the computer.'

Cheryl nodded and led the way back into the corridor. 'Oh, I don't believe it!' she exclaimed. 'This must be Andy's handiwork.'

The monitor screen completely blank and the plug had been pulled out of its socket.

'So we've got to turn it back on,' said Kevin. 'Big deal.'

Don't you understand?' Cheryl answered. 'Nothing was saved. He's rubbed it all off, everything the class has done since we came in. Jacko will go mad.'

Kevin gazed dumbly at the screen.

'I'm going to tell Jacko,' said Cheryl.

Kevin's face twitched. 'Don't.'

'What do you mean, don't?' Cheryl demanded. 'Just look what Brain Damage has done.'

'You're not telling,' Kevin repeated. 'You'll just make things worse. Now leave it.'

Cheryl stared at him in disbelief. 'Are you serious?'

'You still don't get it, do you?' said Kevin. 'If you go running to Jacko, Brain Damage and his mates will take it out on me. And, thanks to you, I'm on my own against them. Now, go to Jacko if you want, but don't you dare mention Brain Damage.'

'You expect me to lie?'

'Cheryl,' Kevin told her simply, 'You owe me one.'

With a sinking heart, Cheryl approached Jacko's desk. 'Mr Jackson.'

He looked up from his marking. 'Yes, Cheryl?'

'It's the computer. We've had a bit of an accident.'

'You've what!'

'I'm sorry. I sort of tripped over the lead. I must have yanked out the plug. I'm sorry.'

Jacko shot out of his chair and stormed into the corridor. 'You've got to be joking,' he shouted. 'The whole morning's work? Oh, for goodness' sake, Cheryl, it's the display for the entrance hall. Didn't you realise how important it was? How could you be so careless?'

The tears were welling up in her eyes. 'I didn't mean it.'

'That isn't the point. I wanted to put it up on the boards tonight.' Jacko frowned as he turned the matter over in his mind. 'Look, you wiped it off. You can type it all out again, every single poem. I don't care if it takes you all morning break and the whole of the lunch hour too. It might teach you not to act silly with school equipment. What about you, Kevin, did you have anything to do with this?'

Cheryl knew what Kevin expected her to say. 'It wasn't Kev, Mr Jackson, it was me.'

As Jacko turned and stamped back into class, Kevin didn't even catch her eye. Not a word of thanks, not a gesture. He just accepted her sacrifice. It was his due.

'OK, Kevin,' she said. 'I owed you and now I've paid you back. But that's it. I'm not going to cover for you any more. You're on your own from now on.'

'So what?' he said dully. 'I always was.'

'I'll tell you this, though,' Cheryl added. 'If you think something like this is going to get Andy off your back, then you must be even more stupid than I thought.'

Kevin just shrugged his shoulders.

Five minutes later the bell rang and everybody filed out into the yard, including Kevin. As Cheryl settled in front of the computer to type out eight poems, each with a different border design, she saw him through the window. He was standing dejectedly by the old bike shed, but she didn't feel a shred of sympathy. It was the first time at Cropper Lane that she'd ever been in trouble. At that moment she hated Kevin as much as everybody else did.

Her bitterness towards Kevin didn't even last out the morning break.

'OK, so speak to me,' said Helen, leaning over Cheryl's shoulder to inspect the computer screen.

'Who said I wasn't?'

'Do you think I'm completely stupid? This is me, Helen, your best friend.'

Cheryl's face must have betrayed her emotions.

'I am still your best friend, aren't I?'

'Are you?'

Helen's face fell. Cheryl recognized the expression. Devastation.

'I didn't mean to let it slip over Kev,' Helen mumbled. 'I don't know what comes over me. My mouth just seems to run away with me.'

'You can say that again,' said Cheryl. Against her natural instincts, she forced herself to be hard and unforgiving.

'I feel terrible,' said Helen. 'I wouldn't hurt Kev for the world. I just didn't think.'

'That makes two of us, and I'm the one who's most to

blame. I dropped Kev in it in the first place. It's no use my blaming you for that.'

'Then what *are* you blaming me for?'

'Think about it. One minute you're all over our Kev. The next you're giving him the cold shoulder. What do you think that's doing to him?'

Helen looked utterly dejected. 'He said that, did he, about me ignoring him?'

Cheryl shook her head. 'Right now, he isn't saying anything to me.'

'That bad, huh?'

'That bad.'

Helen scraped at the ground with the toe of her shoe. 'I can't talk to Kev, though.'

'Why not?'

'Mum told me not to.'

'You mean you blabbed to her, too?'

Helen looked away.

'Oh, Helen! How many more people have you told?'

'I only told one or two,' her friend answered. 'But I think they were all the wrong people. Lots of the parents have been warning their kids off Kev. I know Jamie's dad has.'

Cheryl stared miserably at the computer screen. 'Looks like I've really done it this time,' she groaned.

'Haven't you finished these poems yet?' asked Helen, changing the subject.

'Last one,' said Cheryl. 'How come you're inside, anyway?'

Mrs Wilson asked me to take her cup to the staff-room, so I thought I'd take a little detour to see you.'

'Is Kevin all right?' asked Cheryl.

There was no reply.

'Go on, let's hear it. What's happened?'

'Not much. He's grazed his knee, that's all, and there's a hole in his trouser leg.'

'Andy?'

'Yes, Kevin went to the toilet. Brain Damage and his mates were waiting for him round the corner. They made him run the gauntlet.'

'What about Mrs Wilson?'

'She doesn't use the boys'.'

Cheryl wasn't amused. She was annoyed enough with Helen already.

'This is no time for your stupid jokes. I mean, did she do anything?'

'I don't think she knows about it. Who'd tell her?'

'Poor, stupid Kev,' sighed Cheryl. 'I told him it wouldn't do any good.'

'What?'

'Oh, nothing.'

Helen's lips parted, but the words didn't come out. She had obviously thought better of interrogating Cheryl any further.

'Anyway,' said Helen. 'I'd better go back out before I'm missed.'

'Sure.' said Cheryl shortly. 'You do that.'

Checking the corridor to make sure Jacko wasn't lurking anywhere, she stood up and craned her neck. From the window she could see about half the playground, but there was no sign of either Kevin or Andy. Sliding back into her seat, she started tapping out the final poem.

'How are you doing?' came Jacko's voice a couple of minutes later.

'Sir! You gave me a fright. This is Robert's. It's the last one.'

'Good.' He hovered uncertainly for a moment, then continued: 'Listen, Cheryl, this accident—'

'It was me, Mr Jackson, I tripped over the lead.'

'Yes, so you told me. Are you sure it wasn't more than a simple accident? Mr Hughes has just told me who else was out here with you. I got to thinking that there might be a bit more to it.'

'It was me.'

Jacko rubbed his jaw thoughtfully. 'OK, have it your way, but I can sense that something's going on. We know why Kevin moved schools. If there's anything you want to tell me, don't hesitate.'

'I won't.'

Cheryl watched Jacko retracing his steps to the staffroom, then finished Robert's poem.

'Save As,' she read from the screen. 'Let's see.' She thought for a moment, trying to think of a suitable file name, then typed in the obvious. 'Trouble.'

She had no sooner returned to the main menu, than a whistle blast sounded. Playtime was over. She rocked absent-mindedly on her chair as Mr Hughes' class appeared first. Hughesy himself was at the head of the line. He gave Cheryl a smile and walked into the classroom. Next came the girls, then most of the boys. After a gap, Andy appeared with his mates. Cheryl realised immediately that they must have been waiting for Kevin again. When he finally came into view, her heart sank. In addition to the damage Helen had reported, he was sporting a red mark below the right eye.

'Hello,' Andy announced sarcastically. 'Who's this? It couldn't be the Guv'nor, could it? What's up, Guv, been in the wars?'

Tez led the hoots of approval then bounded jubilantly into class.

'So what happened to you?' asked Cheryl.

'What do you care?'

'Oh, give over feeling sorry for yourself. You know I care.'

Kevin brushed past, lingering for a moment to throw a parting shot. 'Then you've got a funny way of showing it!'

'He isn't going to forgive you easily, is he?' remarked Helen, arriving behind Kevin.

'Heard that, did you?'

Helen nodded.

'How did he get the mark on his face, anyway? He wouldn't tell me.'

'I didn't see. They must have got him on the way back into school. Shoved him against the wall or something.'

'This could get nasty,' said Cheryl.

'Tell me about it! I don't think Brain Damage has even got into his stride yet. They were never more than a few feet away from Kevin all playtime, like a pack of wolves.'

'And he was on his own?'

'Except for Bashir. He hangs around a bit, but Kevin doesn't take any notice. Nobody else will go near.'

'What about you?' Cheryl asked. 'You could stand by him.'

Helen was squirming. 'I told you. My mum would kill me.'

'You want to be friends again?' Cheryl asked. 'Then you help Kev.'

'But Cheryl,' Helen protested. 'That's not fair. It isn't up to me.'

'No excuses,' said Cheryl. 'We come as a package. Me *and* Kev.'

As Helen went into class, Cheryl marvelled at her own toughness. Maybe at last she really did have some of Kev's steel in her. She glanced through the classroom door. The Kev she saw didn't seem to have much steel left, however. He was at his desk, his face buried in his hands. He looked crushed.

Seventeen

*S*O *WHAT DO I DO NOW? I SAW THIS NATURE FILM ONCE.*
*There was this great big spider, a tarantula, I think. He
was surrounded by thousands of ants and they were eating
him alive. It was horrible. I mean, this spider, he was proud,
a hunter. One-on-one he could have killed any of those ants,
but they were all over him and he couldn't move. He just had
to lie there while they destroyed him. It's me, that spider.*

*I'd take any one of those cowards but I'm on my own
against half a dozen and there's nobody standing up for me,
nobody at all. All the kids are keeping their distance. Even the
ones who like me have been ordered off by their parents. The
Guv'nor? Who am I kidding? Why couldn't I keep my big
mouth shut? Cheryl was right about that.*

*I wish I had someone to turn to, but I haven't. Mum's dead
depressed. She's smoking even more than usual. She smells
like an ash-tray. I don't think she can believe it's come out
already. Then there's Jamie, he walks away the moment I go
near him. Helen's the same. As for Cheryl, she's the one who
dropped me in it in the first place.*

*It's even worse than last time. I'm down a dead-end street.
So how's about it, Dad? What would you do? I've got this
memory, of something you did, something big. It's there, at
the back of my mind somewhere. It's like I saw you rip the
whole world wide open in front of me. A big thing, that's what
I need, something that blows them all away. Oh, who am I
kidding? You can't help me; nobody can.*

Maybe there's only one thing I can do. The fire's still there. It burned low for a while, but it's there, all right. Now it's calling me. I hate school. I hate this estate. I hate everything. I want to burn it all down.

Eighteen

'*H*AVE YOU FALLEN OUT WITH HELEN, OR something?'

Cheryl continued to pore over the sports-shop catalogue for her new jogging pants. She didn't turn round.

'No, why?'

Somehow, lying through your teeth gets easier with practice.

'It's the High School Club. Aren't you going with her?'

'I don't know. Maybe I'll give it a miss this week.'

'Don't treat me like I'm stupid, Cheryl. It's all this bother over Kevin, isn't it?'

Cheryl could feel the blood thudding in her temple. 'You know.'

'Of course I know. Carol's been talking about nothing else. I thought you might have confided in me earlier.'

Cheryl lowered her eyes. 'I was too ashamed.'

Her mother squeezed her shoulder. 'Well, it's done now. There's no sense breaking friends over it.'

'Is Aunt Carol angry with me?'

'Well, it hasn't helped, has it? She's disappointed.'

Mum's voice trailed off. Mum and Aunt Carol must have had had words over it.

'I'm sorry.'

'Don't apologize to me,' said Mum. 'If you've got anything to say, save it for Carol. Anyway, what's done is done. You're still young to be carrying that much responsibility. We'll just have to hope it blows over. At least Carol and Kevin don't have to bump into the old fellow's family any more. The move did that much.'

Cheryl didn't feel very reassured by her mother's words. Everybody seemed to be blaming her for telling on Kevin. She'd wrecked the new start. She was too young, a spoilt, little brat who couldn't keep her mouth shut. I've got to do something to put things right, she thought. I've just got to. After a couple of minutes she dropped the catalogue into the newspaper rack and trailed into the kitchen after her mother.

'So where's Dad?'

Mum didn't answer. She didn't need to. The way she was rubbing with that Brillo pad, she was less than overjoyed with him.

'You remember Dad?' Cheryl joked feebly. 'Small, tubby, usually sits in the corner of the living room.'

'He's gone round his mother's.'

You could always tell when Mum and Dad had had a row. Gran's became His Mother's. There was a time when such quarrels came as infrequently as a 61 bus. Not lately, though.

'Why?'

'To get away from me, I suppose. Oh, you may as well know. We've been arguing again.'

'What was it this time?'

Her mother slapped the Brillo pad into the brownish dish-water. 'What's it ever about? He can't stand the thought of living off my wages.' She mimicked Dad's most self-pitying whine. '*It's my pride.*'

'But you don't mind, do you? I mean, it isn't Dad's fault he's lost his job.'

'That's what I keep telling him, but the silly old goat won't listen. He's living in the past. Thinks the man should be the bread-winner, all that stuff. What gets me is, if he's like this after a couple of weeks, what'll he be like when he's actually out of work?'

'I wish you wouldn't argue all the time.'

Her mother smiled wearily. 'Cheryl, that makes two of us. Wipe this lot, will you, love? I'm going to sit down with the *Echo*. It'll do me good to read about a few people worse off than me.'

Cheryl watched her mother settling down at the kitchen table. In the silence that followed, only the tick of the clock could be heard. After a few minutes there was a loud rumble and the hob began to rattle as a train pulled out of the station. Regular, she thought, reliable. So why aren't people?

'Can I go out for a bit?' she asked, wiping the surface and dropping the dishcloth back into the bowl. 'It's still light.'

'OK, but only for an hour.'

Mum tapped her watch and set the deadline.

Cheryl cycled round aimlessly. To be honest, she wasn't going anywhere. She was cycling just to cycle, to clear her head and come up with a solution to the whole, grotesque mess. Life had taken a turn and she didn't like it. Boring she could handle. Routine she positively liked. But this, the feeling of things cracking away at the edges, it was too much. She skirted Kevin's estate. The Diamond was notorious locally. It had the reputation of a rest home for retired psychopaths. Shorn of the exaggerations and inflated tales, it was a grim arrangement of 1960s houses and maisonettes, some abandoned, most of them crumbling visibly. Everything about it – the broken glass, the litter, the abandoned car tyres – announced the hopelessness of the place.

She found herself riding down Kevin's street, Owen Avenue. There was no sign of life at number 15, and what would she have done if there had been? She wasn't exactly top of Kevin's pops just then.

'Cheryl.'

'Oh, hi, Bashir. Where did you spring from?'

'I live here. Number 83.'

Cheryl looked along the row of houses. It seemed crazy. You flee some African civil war, and this is where they stick you.

'Looking for Kevin?' Bashir asked.

'Uh huh.'

'He went out a few minutes ago. I saw him from my window.'

'Oh.'

There didn't seem that much more to say. A painful silence followed.

'Do you want to go and look for him?' Bashir asked hopefully.

Cheryl sensed the boy's loneliness. It was something she could almost touch.

'I think I know where he is,' Bashir added.

'Where?'

'He goes watching Andy Ramage.'

'You serious? He's spying on Brain Damage?'

Bashir nodded. 'His gang is building a fire … a …'

'Bonfire?'

A nod of confirmation.

Cheryl's heart kicked. 'And Kevin's watching them?'

'Is something wrong?'

She slid off her bike and pushed it. 'Show me.'

Bashir led her to the edge of the patch of waste-ground opposite South Road Community Centre.

'Over there,' he said.

It was Andy and Tez they spotted first. They were with a couple of other boys, and they were hauling four splintered, wooden planks behind them.

'So where's Kev?' Cheryl wondered aloud.

Bashir shook his head. 'I can't … No, there he is.'

Kevin had broken cover and darted across a rubble-strewn corner of the field. Meanwhile, Brain Damage's gang stepped back to admire their handiwork.

'So what are you up to?' Cheryl asked, propping her bike against a wall and approaching Kevin from behind.

'You.'

'Who did you expect? The Pope?'

'Are you spying on me?'

'That's rich coming from you.'

Kev snorted. 'Why can't you leave me alone?'

'Come on, Bashir,' said Cheryl. 'Let's leave Sourpuss to it.'

As they turned to go there was a guttural cry. 'McGovern!'

The shout was accompanied by a thrown half-brick.

'That's torn it,' said Cheryl, snatching up her bike. 'Run.'

There was no need to repeat the order for Kevin's benefit. He had already caught up.

'They're gaining,' panted Cheryl. She was tempted to ride off, but it would have meant abandoning Kev and Bashir.

'I'll never make it home,' panted Kevin, as a stone struck the pavement by his foot.

'Your house, no,' said Bashir. 'Mine's nearer.'

'Quick,' Cheryl shouted, dropping her bike in the garden and following the boys into Bashir's. 'Shut the door behind you.'

They heard Andy angrily kicking Bashir's front door. 'We'll have you,' he roared through the letter box. 'All of you.'

Cheryl wasn't sure what it was that woke her, but

something did. She lay in bed for a while, thinking about the narrow squeak with Brain Damage, then sat up. She listened for the night sounds, trying to work out what time it was.

'Easy,' she told herself presently. 'Dead easy.'

There were so many tell-tale clues; the regular slamming of the car doors, the merry, raucous voices of drinkers on their way home, the faint thump of a neighbour's CD player.

'Half past eleven,' she guessed. 'Maybe quarter to twelve.'

It was only then that she turned to examine the digital display of her alarm clock. 11:48. Clever girl!

She was puzzled, though. This wasn't like her at all. She was normally out like a light until morning.

Might as well use the bathroom, she thought. It was only as she padded along the landing that her sense of unease grew. She paused by her parents' bedroom door. It was open. That's what caught her attention. And there was something else; the curtains weren't drawn. She could see her father silhouetted in the moonlight by the window. She might have spoken to him, had she not heard a sound from below.

'That you, Mum?' she whispered, creeping downstairs.

Her mother was at the kitchen table, chin propped on her hands. She was in her dressing gown. Cheryl stole a glance at the shiny booklet lying in front of her mother. *Prospectus*, it read. *John Moores University*.

'Are you all right?'

Her mother's answer sent a shudder down her spine. 'No, love. I'm afraid not.'

'Dad?'

'Uh huh.'

'What was it this time?'

She held up the prospectus. 'I showed him this. I wanted to do a computer course. They suggested it at work. Well, he hit the roof, didn't he? Do you know what he said: *So you swan off on your fancy course and leave me to rot*. He isn't the only one with a life!'

'He'll come round,' said Cheryl.

'Sure of that?'

'Dunno really.'

Her mother reached out and squeezed Cheryl's hand. 'The way he's going,' Mum said, 'he's going to wreck everything. Everything.'

Nineteenth

*S*O THEY THINK THEY'VE GOT ME ON THE RUN, DO
*they? Well, so what if I did leg it tonight? Thanks to
Bashir, I live to fight another day. Brain Damage had better
not make too much of one little victory, though. I've got plans,
Dad, you just see if I haven't. At the moment, it's just an idea,
but I think it might work. I gave Rooster a ring from a call
box, and he's interested. I had to borrow some money from
Mum's purse to do it. She'd go off her head if she knew, but
I'm past caring. I'm on my own. The only person who's
helped me is Bashir, and he'd be no use in a fight. He's puny,
half Brain Damage's size. I bet even fatty Tez could lick the
poor little runt. I don't know why he keeps hanging round me.
What does he want? No, there's only one person who'll stand
by me now, and that's Rooster.*

*He'll help me get Brain Damage off my back. I tried
ignoring him, but would he leave me alone? Oh no, he had to
rub my nose in it. Now he spends half an hour yelling and
lobbing stones at my bedroom window. That's right, they
came back the moment I left Bashir's. I was lucky to make it
up the road. Mum tried to chase them, but they just gave her a
load of verbal. Now I'm under siege in my own home!
Anyway, I'll tell you one thing, Brain Damage is a fool to
himself. If he'd had the sense to lay off, maybe my revenge
wouldn't have been too bad. I might have gone easy on him.
Not now, not now.*

No, my revenge is going to be terrible. I've already got the idea. I just need somebody to help me put it into action. Rooster will know what to do. He always does.

Twenty

'OH, COME ON,' HELEN PLEADED. 'YOU'VE BEEN keeping it up all week. Look, it's Friday already. Can't we make it up in time for the week-end. Give me a break, eh?'

'I will,' said Cheryl.

'You will?'

'That's right. All you've got to do is make up with Kev.'

'I can't.'

'I don't believe you. Can't you see how upset he is?'

'How many more times,' Helen replied. 'My mum would kill me.'

'You used to be his biggest fan,' said Cheryl. 'A real friend would stick by him.'

'Maybe you ought to practise what you preach,' Helen retorted. 'I don't see you talking to him.'

'*He* won't talk to *me*,' Cheryl declared. 'He still blames me for everything that's happened.'

She and Helen were standing at the school gates. For Kevin, it had been another day of crawling over barbed wire. First there had been his maths book, scribbled on on every page. Then he'd been cornered in the toilets and slammed repeatedly against the wall. Finally, he'd been completely cold-shouldered in games, left to mark out the touchline by himself. And every single time, he'd had to face Brain Damage and his gang. Alone.

'Listen, Cheryl,' Helen said. 'I can't do it. I just can't. I promised.'

'Like you promised to keep Kev's secret?'

Helen's face wore a pained expression. For a moment, Cheryl almost felt sorry for her, but the sight of Kevin trudging miserably out of school reminded her of what he was suffering.

'Here's your chance,' she said.

Helen shook her head. 'I told you; I can't.'

'Won't is more like it.'

With that, Cheryl fell in behind Kevin. She knew he wouldn't let her walk with him, so she plodded along the road, keeping him in sight.

'Can't I at least walk with you?' called Helen from the gates.

'It's a free country,' Cheryl answered. She didn't really mind at all; she'd been missing her friend's company. She was sure her stand against Helen's spinelessness was right, but why was the right thing always so tough? It was hurting her as much as Helen. Without another word, she allowed Helen to join her and the two of them trailed silently after Kevin. They had almost reached the crossroads where he turned right for the Diamond and Cheryl took a left, when Helen stiffened.

'What's up with you?' Cheryl asked.

'Across the road,' Helen whispered. 'No, not there. Up ahead, waiting for Kev.'

It was Andy. He was accompanied by Tez and two more of his gang.

'I'd better warn him,' said Cheryl.

'No point,' Helen told her. 'He already knows.'

Sure enough, Kev had slowed down. He hovered uncertainly round the chippy on Irene Avenue, then started to run. Andy's mates were right behind him.

'Come on,' yelled Cheryl.

'What can we do?' asked Helen.

'I don't know, but we've got to do something.'

Tez was yelling threats, but Kev had a good start.

'He's losing them,' panted Helen.

'Looks like it,' Cheryl answered.

They had to wait for traffic to pass on the main road, before resuming the chase.

'They've gone,' cried Cheryl.

'No,' said Helen. 'Look, there.'

Kevin was half-way along the main road. Two more blocks and he would reach the edge of the Diamond.

'He's going to make it,' said Cheryl.

'He's a born survivor,' said Helen.

Cheryl slowed to a walk. 'You can say that again.'

The girls were about to go, when Cheryl glanced back. 'Hang on a minute. Where's Brain Damage vanished to?'

'I don't know.'

'And what's Kev stopped for?'

The answer wasn't long coming. Andy suddenly materialized out of an alley-way.

'So that's where he went,' Cheryl said grimly. 'He must have gone across the waste-ground to cut Kev off.'

Kevin was standing at the street corner. Andy was approaching from one direction and his three mates from the other. Cheryl knew what he was thinking. He could still beat Brain Damage, but by the time he'd taken out Andy his mates would be on top of him. His hesitation was to cost him dear.

'McGovern!' yelled Andy.

The shout was a signal to the others. They cannoned into Kev, sending him sprawling on the pavement. Hopelessly outnumbered, he rolled up in a ball, his arms wrapped round his head. Ramage's crew were all over him, kicking and stamping. The force of one kick made Kevin spin. He looked so pathetic, knees curled against his chest, face buried between his arms, taking it, just taking it.

'Stop it!' shrieked Helen.

Cheryl did more than cry out. She'd never had a fight in her life, not a real one. But there was Kev, a helpless bundle being pummelled and kicked like he was just a bunch of rags. He didn't deserve it. No matter what he'd done, he was better than any of them. He was worth the risk. She started to run in the boys' direction. Tez's elbow caught her full in the face, but she barely even flinched. She wasn't going to cry like a spoilt brat. She could make a difference. Soon, she and Helen were struggling to pull them off. Suddenly the fight was halted by the squeal of car brakes.

'Hey, knock it off!'

It was Hughesy.

'Andrew Ramage, come here.'

Andy and his friends were in no mood to obey. They took to their heels and were out of sight in a matter of seconds.

'Andrew!'

Hughesy shook his head, then bent down to examine Kevin. 'How do you feel, son?'

Kevin accepted a helping hand and rose groggily to his feet.

'Is he all right, Sir?' asked Cheryl.

'Yes,' said Hughesy. 'You'll live, won't you, Kevin?'

'I'm OK.'

Without a word of thanks, Kevin limped away.

'Don't worry about Kevin, Mr Hughes,' said Cheryl, noticing the teacher's look of surprise. 'He's like that.'

'Do you know what all this was about?' asked Hughesy. 'It was a pretty nasty attack. If I hadn't been passing, Kevin might have been badly hurt.'

Cheryl knew Kevin wouldn't thank her for dragging Hughesy in. 'They just don't like each other.'

'Well, I'll be having a word with those three about their behaviour on Monday morning. See you.'

'Yes, see you, Mr Hughes.'

'It's lucky he showed,' said Helen.

'Not half. Come on, Brain Damage might still be around.'

They soon discovered Kevin. He was dusting himself down and examining his reflection in the advertising panel of a bus shelter. He pulled out a grimy handkerchief, licked it and dabbed gingerly at his face. Satisfied with the result, he moved off.

'Are you all right, Kev?' asked Cheryl.

'You a comedian, or something?' Kevin snapped.

'We only wanted to see if you were OK,' Helen explained.

'Well I am, so now you can leave me in peace.' With that he stamped away down Owen Avenue. They watched as he crashed angrily into the house and slammed the door behind him.

'Do you think Brain Damage has finished with him?' Helen wondered out loud.

'I doubt it,' Cheryl answered. 'There's more in store yet.'

'Maybe we should have talked to Hughesy about it.'

'No, Kevin wouldn't want that. It's up to him now.'

'Poor Kev. What do you think he's going to do?'

Cheryl shrugged her shoulders. Of one thing she was sure, Kevin might lie down and take it for a day, maybe even a week, then he would find a way to hit back. She was suddenly very scared.

'I'm sorry I didn't stick up for Kev before,' Helen added. 'I won't let him down again.'

Cheryl smiled, remembering the way Helen had flung herself into the battle. 'I know you won't.'

'Friends again?' asked Helen.

'Yes, friends.'

Twenty-One

*A*UNT PAT CALLED ROUND LAST NIGHT. HER AND Cheryl. Well, Mum starts giving Cheryl the third degree, doesn't she? How did I get in this state? Wasn't she supposed to look out for me in this new school? That sort of thing. It was quite funny, really. You'd think Cheryl had beaten me up, the way Mum went on at her. So that gets Mum and Aunty Pat at each other's throats. Don't talk to Cheryl like that, says Aunty Pat. It was a real ding dong for a few minutes. I thought Cheryl was going to burst into tears. I don't feel sorry for her, though. It'll probably do her good seeing me get roughed up. Now she knows what her stupid mouth has done to me.

Anyway, in the end Mum and Aunty Pat told each other they were sorry and made it up, which is more than I did with Cheryl. And guess what? They're going to take us to a firework display, the big one in the park. I've seen all the preparations. There's a big chain-link fence and all the proper stuff for launching the rockets. Everybody says it's brilliant, one of the best in the North West.

But I've been planning my own little bonfire party. I phoned Rooster again. He's game for a bit of fun. In fact, he knows where to get all the gear to make it go off with a bang. You can rely on Rooster. Nobody ever has a good word for him, but I'll tell you what, whenever my back's against the wall, he always comes through for me. I don't care what any of them say; Mum, the teachers, my social worker, Rooster's *the one who's always stuck by me. Nobody else is going to help me.*

That's it, then. If I want a life I'm going to have to do something, and I know the very thing. I'm going to make people sit up and take notice. And how!

Twenty-Two

*C*HERYL COULD FEEL EVERYBODY LOOKING AT her as she slipped into class.

'You late too, Cheryl?' asked Jacko. 'I don't suppose you know why Kevin's off.'

Cheryl glanced at his place. Sure enough, it was empty. 'No,' she replied. 'I've no idea.'

And for once, she didn't give a damn where he was. She had more important things on her mind.

'Oh, I'll mark him absent.' Jacko closed the register. 'Right, then, seeing as you're here you may as well take it up to the office.'

Cheryl stared dumbly at the proferred register.

'The register,' Jacko explained. 'I'd like you to take it to the secretary for me.'

'Oh, yes I will.'

'Is everything all right?' asked Jacko.

'Yes,' Cheryl answered, unable to disguise the slight shake in her voice. 'I'm fine.'

As she turned to go, she met Helen's eyes. It was as if her friend could see right into her heart. Once out of the door, she gave a long, shuddering sigh. *Is everything all right?* Of course it wasn't. It might just be that nothing would ever be right again. She'd discovered the truth the night before, between the end of *Brookside* and bedtime. Dad had gone. To 'His Mother's'. And this time it wasn't for a visit. He would be staying there. How did Mum put it? For a while.

'Thanks, Dad,' she hissed under her breath as she walked the empty corridor. 'Thanks for everything.'

She remembered Mum's college prospectus. Had that done it, something so simple? Her memories lined up, and one memory mocked her more than all the others. *I'll give you a promise right now. Come what may, I'm not going anywhere.*

Well, he'd gone, all right. Without a word. Like a thief in the night. It was so dishonest, to go like that, unannounced. He was a coward, a liar, and she hated him.

'Is that for me, Cheryl?' She'd arrived at the Secretary's office without realising.

'Oh, sorry, Mrs Poulton.'

'Are you all right, love?'

It was the second time somebody had said that in five minutes. Cheryl bit her lip. I must look a right state, she thought.

'Yes, I'm OK. Bit of a bug, that's all.'

'Well, I'm not so sure you should be in. There are some bad viruses around. Our Richard was in bed for a fortnight with one.'

Cheryl listened to Mrs Poulton droning on about viruses, and legs like jelly, and how medicine didn't seem to clear them up the way it used to and all the while she wanted to scream. Never before in her life had she felt so low.

'So you take care of yourself,' she heard the Secretary conclude.

'Don't worry,' Cheryl replied, relieved to escape. 'I will.'

On the way back to class, she nipped into the toilets. She examined her face in the mirror. The eyes which stared back were red-rimmed with crying. A virus, that was a good name for it!

'Kev's still not here,' said Helen, as Cheryl slid into her seat.

'Well, I haven't seen him!'

Her reply was a whiplash.

Helen gave her a startled look, as if to say: Now, what's that in aid of? I thought we'd made it up. 'You all right?'

'Not you as well. That's all anybody's said to me this morning.'

Jacko was listening to Karen Jarman read, a finger pressed to his temple, while the rest of the class got on with their maths.

'Sorry I spoke,' Helen grumbled. 'You don't have to bite my head off.'

Cheryl pursed her lips. 'It isn't you. Things at home.'

Jacko looked up to carry out one of his periodic sweeps of the class. 'Jamie,' he warned. 'Get on with your work.' Satisfied that he was again occupied listening to Karen, Cheryl continued. 'I'll tell you at break.'

Helen nodded and copied a sum from the board, before pausing. 'There is something you should know, though,' she said. 'It's Kev. I saw him this morning. He had his uniform on and everything. I'm sure it was him.'

Cheryl frowned. For a second, her own worries slipped to the back of her mind. 'So why isn't he in?' she mused aloud.

Exactly what I was wondering,' said Helen.

They were interrupted by Jacko. 'Right,' he said, ushering Karen back to her place. 'Close your books.'

'But, Sir,' came a complaint, 'I haven't finished.'

'You have now,' said Jacko. 'I told you it was a speed test. I'll mark what you've done so far.'

He waited until all the maths books had been handed

in, then picked up a sheaf of papers from his desk. 'Karen,' he said. 'Hand these out, please.'

Cheryl stared at the street map in front of her.

'Now,' Jacko continued. 'If you've quite finished talking, Jamie Moore, we'll get on.'

A scowl from Jamie.

'I want you to chart your journey home from school on the map,' Jacko explained. 'You've got a highlighter pen to mark the route. Once you have done that, there are further instructions on the back of the map. We went over this last week, so you should be able to get on with it yourselves while I look through some reading folders.'

Cheryl picked out Kevin's house, then her own. Then slowly, her finger traced out County Road until she came to the edge of the map. Her finger ran on. She found herself examining a mark that a previous pupil had gouged into the desk. If the map had been big enough, that mark was about where Kevin's old estate would have been.

'What are you doing?' asked Helen.

'I've got this feeling,' said Cheryl. 'It's just a hunch.'

'Go on, what?'

Cheryl shook her head. 'It's probably nothing.'

'You always say that,' Helen complained. 'Every time Kevin gets mentioned; it's nothing.'

Just then, two Year Five girls knocked and entered. 'Please, Mr Jackson,' one of them stammered, 'Mrs Harrison wants to see Kevin McGovern.'

'I'm afraid he's not in this morning, girls.'

They turned to go, then stopped. 'Oh, she asked for Cheryl Tasker as well.'

'Cheryl? OK, I'll send her.'

She knocked on Mrs Harrison's door.

'Come in. Ah, Cheryl. Sit down. Don't look so scared; you're not in any trouble.'

Cheryl sat on the chair furthest from the Head's desk.

'Come on, now. I won't bite. Here.'

Reluctantly, she moved.

'Now, tell me what happened on Friday afternoon.'

Cheryl twisted her long-suffering lock of hair.

'Mr Hughes reported a fight between your cousin and a number of other boys.'

'It wasn't a fight, Miss, they jumped him. He didn't stand a chance.'

'And do you know what it was all about?'

'I don't know. Maybe it's because he's new.'

Mrs Harrison observed Cheryl sceptically. 'That isn't quite how Mr Jackson and Mr Hughes see it. They tell me he settled in well at first. A popular boy, they tell me. So why the sudden change?'

Cheryl didn't know how to answer. How could she admit that she'd ratted on him? 'I don't know, Miss.'

'And you don't know where he is this morning?'

'No, Miss.'

They were interrupted by a firm rap at the door.

'That'll be Andrew Ramage and his friends,' said Mrs Harrison. 'Let them in on your way out. And Cheryl ...'

'Yes, Miss.'

'If you have second thoughts, don't hesitate to come and see me.'

'No, Miss.'

As she left the Head's office she almost bumped into Andy.

'Where's the Guv'nor this morning?' he sniped. 'Can't stand the heat, eh?'

'I'll give you heat, Andrew Ramage,' came Mrs Harrison's voice. 'Come in here at once.'

Leaving Andy to his interrogation, Cheryl escaped back to class.

'Well?'

'It was about Friday.'

'Did you say anything?'

'No, I kept my mouth shut. It's what I should have done in the first place.'

'Helen, Cheryl,' Jacko said from his desk. 'Settle down and get on with your maps.'

Returning to the map in front of her, Cheryl found her own problems overshadowing thoughts of Kevin. She began to trace a new route. It led from her house to her Gran's. And Dad.

Twenty-Three

FREE, THAT'S WHAT I FEEL. NO, BETTER THAN FREE. I'M the Guv'nor. There's me and the fire and I'm its master. Brain Damage might not know it, but I'm on his case. I've been watching him. I've got it off to a fine art. It's like I'm invisible, the ghost that haunts Andy Ramage. I'm building up a picture of his movements. I know what he does and when he does it. He's a fish on a line, and I'm about to reel him in. After this nobody will dare mess with me. If anybody so much as looks at me, I'll have them. I've had enough of being bottom of the pile. Who wants to be a licking boy all their life? You never were. People seem to think they can do anything to me, and I'll just take it. Well, I'll show them. They're not going to forget who my dad is. The hard man's son, that's who I am. I'm going to pay them back. Every one of them.

I almost feel sorry for Brain Damage and his gang. They think I'm finished. They think it's back to the old days. Well, boys, you'd better enjoy it while you can because tomorrow night I'm going to bring you right back down to earth with a bump. No, better than that, a bang. It is Bonfire Night, after all.

They didn't go straight home tonight. I didn't really expect them to. They're building a bonfire on the waste-ground at the back of the estate. They're full of it. 'It's going to be a great bommy night,' that's what Brain Damage keeps saying. Now, who am I to disagree? I'm sure they won't mind me and Rooster gate-crashing the party, especially when we're bringing along our own fireworks. Rooster says they're really special.

I can't wait to see Brain Damage's face, I just can't wait.

Twenty-Four

'H<small>E'LL COME BACK THOUGH, WON'T HE</small>?'
Cheryl was standing by the shops on Irene Avenue, her swimming things tucked under her arm. There was a time when she would have sobbed her heart out over something like Dad's departure, but that was one thing she'd learned from Kev, how to cry inside. You don't show how you feel. You hold it back while you think how to fight back against the pain. You let it smoulder where nobody can see. Kev had put some of his fire inside her. He said it with every beat of his heart: You don't have to take it.

'I mean,' Helen continued. 'He's a good dad, isn't he? He wouldn't just clear off.'

'Your guess is as good as mine, Helen. He phoned me last night.'

'What did he say?'

'Not much. It was like we were strangers. I thought I had it all worked out. I'd got this big speech all prepared in my head. Then the phone goes and it's Dad on the other end. So what happens? My mind just goes blank. It was the most important conversation of my life, and I talked gibberish. You know what we ended up talking about – the weather!'

Helen nodded sympathetically.

'I mean, it's just so stupid. Mum doesn't want him to move out, and I know he doesn't want to. It's like he wants to hurt himself, to say sorry for losing his job. And that's another thing, he hasn't even been finished yet. He's still working out his redundancy. Imagine what he'll be like when he's actually on the dole!'

Helen slung her bag over her shoulder. 'We're not going to sort anything out, hanging round here. Let's get off to the baths. I've got to be home by half past four.'

'Yes, same here.'

'You could always go and see your dad,' Helen suggested.

'Do you think it would help?'

'He's your dad. You tell me.'

'I don't know. It's all so confusing.'

'But you've just told me he doesn't want to go.'

'That's right.'

'And you're sure your mum wants him back?'

'Yes.'

'Then go and see him. What harm can it do?'

Cheryl smiled. Helen was right of course. Right like 5+5=10 is right. Right like black is black and white is white is right. The trouble was, life didn't have that sort of right and wrong any more. She'd always thought of life like a game board. There were squares you went on and squares where you weren't allowed. That's why Kevin scared her so much. He just wouldn't stick to the rules. He was the boy who climbed the snakes and slid down the ladders. The things that happened to him weren't supposed to happen to anyone.

'So have you made up your mind?'

'I don't know, Helen. Honestly I don't. I can't go tonight, anyway. It's that big bonfire at the park. You're still coming, aren't you?'

'Of course I am, but what about your dad, what *are* you going to do?'

Suddenly, it was the old Cheryl speaking. It was one

thing to find the courage to tackle the school bullies. It was quite another to try and sort out your parents' lives for them. 'It's hard, Helen.' she said. 'Maybe I should just leave it to them to sort out.'

'They haven't got much of a track record so far,' Helen observed wryly.

Cheryl let the comment pass and stopped at the kerb to await a break in the traffic.

'Hello,' said Helen, joining her. 'Look who's here.'

Cheryl turned. Kevin was trying to cross the road from the other side, staggering under the weight of a large package wrapped in a black bin-bag. He was dodging the traffic.

'Where did he appear from?' asked Cheryl.

'Got off the bus, I think. See, there's one just going.'

'That one? If it's the twenty-one he got off, then I've a good idea what he's been sagging school for.'

That's when Cheryl became aware of somebody gesturing to Kevin from the opposite pavement. He too was carrying something bulky in a bin-bag.

'I knew it!'

'What's up?'

'That lad,' Cheryl replied. 'The one Kevin's shouting at. That's Rooster.'

'Who?'

'Don't tell me you've forgotten. The trouble-maker Kev lit the fire with.'

Now she had Helen's attention. 'So that's him.'

'That's him, all right. But what are they up to?'

'No idea,' said Helen, 'But I'd love to know what that is they're carrying.'

'So would I.'

'Come on, Rooster,' Kevin was shouting. 'You can't hang round here all day, you know. Make a dash for it.'

'Get lost,' Rooster yelled above the roar of the traffic. 'You're going to get us both killed.'

'The car hasn't been built that can get the Guv'nor,' Kevin boasted. With that, he ran the rest of the way across the road, earning himself a few blasts on the horn from angry drivers. 'Pull your finger out, Roost. What's up, turned chicken?'

Snarling at the joke, Rooster eventually managed to negotiate the busy road and join Kevin.

Cheryl decided to take the bull by the horns, or was it the Rooster by the wings? 'What brings you up this end, Rooster?' she asked, confronting them.

Kevin looked surprised. 'Cheryl!'

'That's right.'

'What are you doing here?'

'We were on our way to the baths after school,' she answered. 'You do remember school?'

'Don't try to be clever,' said Kev.

'What's in the bin-bags?' asked Helen.

'Nothing.'

'Pretty big nothings.'

Rooster chuckled. 'We've already brought up two big nothings today, haven't we, Kev?'

Kevin whipped round. If looks could kill!

'Well?' Cheryl asked.

'Well what?'

'What have you got?'

'You don't expect me to tell, do you?'

'Suit yourself,' said Cheryl.

'Thanks,' Kevin told her. 'We will.'

'Do you think it's worth following them?' asked Helen as the boys walked away.

Cheryl watched them uncertainly for a few moments, then shook her head. 'No. They'll just keep wandering about till we get fed up.'

—— 123 ——

'I won't get fed up,' said Helen.

'Well, I will. I've got better things than our Kev to worry about.'

'Maybe you're right,' said Helen, grudgingly. Despite everything, she still had a crush on Kevin. 'I just wish I knew what they were planning.'

'Well,' Cheryl sighed. 'They're not going to let on, are they?'

They walked in silence for a while, then Helen stopped.

'What now?'

'Your Kevin,' said Helen. 'You don't think he's up to his old tricks, do you?'

'I hope not.'

'But you *are* worried.'

Cheryl pulled nervously at her hair. A few bangers were going off prematurely in the distance, and from somewhere on the Diamond there was the smell of burning.

'What do you think?'

Twenty-Five

THERE WAS A SURPRISE WAITING FOR CHERYL when she got back from the baths. Mum and Aunt Carol were in the kitchen talking. The whole room stank of tobacco smoke. It wasn't difficult to guess what they were discussing. The moment Cheryl walked in they started talking loudly about the sale at T. J. Hughes. It was a dead giveaway. So was the fact that while Gareth was kneeling on the floor, playing with his spacemen, his big brother was nowhere to be seen.

'Where's Kev?' asked Cheryl, immediately fearing the worst.

'Upstairs in your room,' said Mum. 'I said he could have a go on your Amiga.'

Cheryl flew upstairs. Her days of sugar and spice were over. She was going to have it out with him for once and for all.

'What do you think you're doing, Kev?' she demanded. 'You can't just pretend school doesn't exist. You must know they're going to start asking questions. And what if your mum finds out?'

'Who cares?' Kevin grunted, looking round her room with a bored expression. 'They might find out, but not for a while yet. That's unless you're thinking of blowing me up to Mrs Harrison now.'

'Oh, give me strength!'

Kevin crossed the room. 'It is your speciality, isn't it? Ratting on people.'

Cheryl grabbed his sleeve. 'Listen you. I don't have to take this.'

Kevin shrugged her off. 'Suit yourself. But keep your mitts off.' He had reached the door of her room. 'I'm going to see if it's time to go,' he told her. 'I'm sick of hanging round this dump, listening to you whinging.'

Cheryl's eyes were stinging, with indignation more than anything. 'Look, Kev, I know what you've been up to.'

He paused.

'That's right. I know why you've been bunking off school.'

'You think you do.'

Cheryl was struggling to keep her temper. 'Can't you see I'm trying to help?'

'Of course you are,' he retorted bitterly. 'That's why you blabbed to Helen, isn't it?'

Cheryl refused to be side-tracked. 'I saw those packages, remember. I know you've got something planned. Does it have anything to do with Andy Ramage?'

Kevin's eyes narrowed. 'You don't know what you're talking about.'

'No? Then what are you getting so hot under the collar about?'

At last she'd broken through the wall of hostility he'd built. She had him on the defensive.

'You're going to do something stupid, I just know it.'

Kevin recovered quickly. His answer was accompanied by a sneer of contempt. 'Stupid, is it? I'll tell you one thing, after tonight everything will be sorted.'

Cheryl froze for a moment. A tremor ran through her. 'What do you mean?'

Kevin turned his back. 'Wouldn't you just like to

know.' He opened the door. 'I'm going to chase Mum up. I don't have to listen to you rambling on.'

Cheryl pursued him down the stairs. 'Don't do it, Kev, whatever it is. Please.'

'Get off my back, will you?'

Cheryl followed him helplessly into the kitchen.

'Are we going yet?' he demanded.

Aunt Carol glanced at her watch. 'In a minute, love. Go and get Gareth for me. He's just gone out on the climbing frame.' She switched her attention to Cheryl's mum. 'Right, sis, we'd better make tracks. What time does this display start?'

'Eight.'

'So we'll be back round about half past seven. It'll give us time to have a bite of tea and dig out the wellies. That park will be a quagmire after all the rain we've had.'

'About half past seven, then.'

Gareth arrived from the garden up to his knees in mud.

'See what I mean about wellies,' said Aunt Carol. 'Come on, mischief. We'll go round the back way so we don't walk mud through the house.'

Cheryl watched Kevin trail out after his mum. Tonight, he said. It was going to happen tonight. But how? He'd be at the display with them. Maybe it was all talk after all. One thing was for certain, she wasn't going to take her eyes off him all night.

As Cheryl listened to the entry door slam, her mind switched to other matters. After all, she didn't need to worry about Kev for a couple of hours. She made a sudden decision and turned to her mother. 'Can I go round Helen's?'

'What, now?'

'Yes.'

'But you've only just walked home with her.'

Cheryl was thinking on her feet. 'I think I told her the wrong time for the display. She'll be too late.'

'Why don't you just phone?'

'And I brought her towel back with me by mistake.'

'That can wait till later.'

'But mum …'

Her mother began to smile. 'Listen, Cheryl, I was your age once. I know how much you enjoy Helen's company. I'm just glad you've patched things up. I don't need all these cock and bull excuses. If you want to go round to her house for a while, I don't mind at all. Just make sure you're both back here in plenty of time for the display.'

Cheryl couldn't believe her luck. Mum must be in one of her best moods. A real A+. Without another word, she bolted out of the door and dragged her bike out of the garden shed. She had to act quickly, before her courage deserted her.

'Going Mum,' she called.

'OK, love. Careful on that road.'

At the top of the Avenue, Cheryl paused. Helen's house was to the right. With a smile at the quality of her lying, she turned left. As she pedalled down the hill, she was muttering the same phrase over and over: 'There but for fortune.'

'Cheryl!'

'Hi, Gran. Is Dad in?'

'He's out the back, fixing my guttering. It's come away.'

'Can I go through?'

'Of course you can. Wheel your bike into the hall.' Gran peered out into the street. 'Your mum not with you?'

'She doesn't know I'm here.'

'I see.'

Cheryl found her father coming down the ladder. 'All done, Mam,' he said, hearing the back door opening. 'Oh, Cheryl, it's you.'

She glared at him. 'It's Bonfire Night.' She spoke the words as a challenge.

'Yes,' he said, puzzled. 'I know.'

'I thought you'd come. Like birthdays and Christmas. A time we should all be together.'

'You make it sound like I've been away ages. It's only a couple of days.'

'I know how long it's been. Why did you go?'

'It'd take too long to explain.'

'How long? Longer than it took to make your promise?'

He looked blank.

'*Come what may,*' she reminded him. '*I'm not going anywhere.*'

'Oh,' he said. 'That.'

'Yes, that.'

Her father shifted his feet uneasily.

'Well,' she said. 'If you didn't mean it, why say it?'

'Things change.'

'What things?' Cheryl demanded, tears starting in her eyes, 'Do I matter? Does Mum?'

'Yes, you know you do.'

'Have we done anything wrong?'

'No, of course not. It's me.'

Cheryl ran her hand impatiently down the ladder. 'Are you happier here?'

'No, but—'

'Then come home.'

'It isn't as simple as that.'

'Why not?' The eyes she turned on him were full of rage. She was so angry with him. She hated his weak, whining voice. She hated the stupid squirming. She wanted him the way he used to be. When he carried her on his shoulders and showed her the Mersey and told her about the days when the ships queued up to be berthed. When he took her to Everton games and told her about a great player he called the Golden Vision. When he cuddled her and told her she was his whole world and a bit extra too. She wanted him invincible again.

'I just feel as if I'm no good for anything any more. I've always had work. I mean, what the hell am I for if I haven't got a job?'

'You're my dad!'

'I've got to be more than that, girl. It isn't enough.'

'It's enough for me, and Mum.' She was choked with tears. She started to back away.

'Cheryl, just listen to me for a moment.'

Listen! The time for listening was past.

'Why, are you coming home?'

'No, not yet—'

'Then why should I listen?'

And that was it. She despised herself for coming, for pleading with him. When Helen had suggested it, it had all seemed so easy. Go and see him. Bring him home. She had pictured herself leading her shame-faced father into the living room. She had felt the hugs and kisses of her parents and bathed in the gratitude of them both. But it hadn't been easy at all. He hadn't even listened to her.

'Cheryl!'

She fled down the hall, leaving him calling after her.

'Off so soon?' asked Gran, poking her head out of the living-room door.

'See you, Gran.' There was no disguising the sob in her voice. She bundled her bike out of the door.

'Cheryl, are you all right?' She didn't answer and she didn't look back. She knew what she would have seen, Dad and Gran watching her from the doorstep.

By the time she'd reached the traffic lights, Cheryl's mind had begun to clear. She had decided to call for Helen on the way home. Then it would only be a little white lie she'd told Mum. Now, with Helen in tow, she was heading back.

'Oh, that's all I need,' she said, recognizing a familiar group. They were crossing the railway bridge by St Mary's Church when they saw them; Andy Ramage and his friends dragging a large plank across the waste-ground to their bonfire.

'Just ignore them,' said Helen.

'Hey, Cheryl,' Andy shouted. 'Come over here. We could do with a guy.'

'Yes,' said Tez. 'Nothing like a bit of human sacrifice.'

'No,' said a third boy. 'Tell her to send McGovern down instead.'

'McGovern?' Andy answered. 'He'd be no use as a guy. He's had all the stuffing knocked out of him.'

'Oh, knock it off, Andy,' said Cheryl over the peals of laughter.

She and Helen watched them wedging the plank into position, then continued towards Cheryl's house. As they turned the corner, Andy and his mates crossed the top of the road behind them.

'Why don't you come to our bommy?' shouted Tez. 'There'll be no adults to spoil the fun.'

'No,' Helen shouted. 'Just you boneheads.'

'Forget about them,' said Cheryl. 'We've got the display.'

At least, that's what she thought until she arrived home. No sooner had she walked through the door than she was confronted by her mother and Aunt Carol.

'Have you seen our Kev?' demanded Aunt Carol.

'Kevin?' asked Cheryl. 'But I thought he was with you.'

'He's done a bunk,' said Aunt Carol. 'He's gone.'

'He can't be far,' Cheryl said reassuringly.

The trouble was, the smell of burning was already in her nostrils.

Twenty-Six

*E*VERYTHING IS IN PLACE. THE DRIZZLE HAS STOPPED and it's a fine, dry night. I was having kittens when the rain started. I thought for a few minutes that all my planning was going to go to waste, but now it's perfect. The moon is out and the sky is full of little, blazing stars. A perfect night for it.

Me and Rooster have been guarding Brain Damage's bonfire like it's our own. We can't have anything happening to it now, not with our little secret hidden inside. Now, it's just a matter of waiting. Soon they'll be back to light it, and that'll be it. The moment they let my friend fire out of his box, I'll have them. I'll get my own back for everything they've done. I will be the fire and I'll make them burn.

It's going to be a night to remember.

Twenty-Seven

'JUST WAIT TILL I GET MY HANDS ON HIM,' SAID Aunt Carol. 'I'll kill the little sod!'

Her words didn't carry any conviction. She wasn't angry, she was worried. And to make things worse, she was out of cigarettes.

'Calm down, Carol,' Cheryl's mum advised. 'You'll only get yourself into a state.'

Get herself into a state! Aunt Carol had already gone ballistic.

'But, Pat, I'm scared. After last time—'

'Look,' Mum interrupted, 'There's no sense jumping to conclusions.' She turned to Cheryl and Helen. 'Have either of you got any ideas?'

Aunt Carol looked at them hopefully.

'Well.' Cheryl began uncertainly.

'Please,' begged Aunt Carol. 'Anything.'

'Carol,' Mum said. 'Just let me deal with it, will you?'

Aunt Carol hugged Gareth tightly and sat on the edge of her chair, listening.

'Go on, love,' said Mum, 'If you know anything at all, you'll have to tell us.'

'I don't think it would do any good,' Cheryl said. 'The mood he's in, he won't listen to adults.'

'We'll have to make him listen.'

'There might be a better way,' Cheryl suggested.

'What?'

'Let me and Helen go and look for him. Alone.'

'I'm not sure about that,' said her mother. 'I don't like the idea of you wandering around in the dark.'

'Please, Mum. We won't be wandering about. I've got a good idea where he is, but if he sees you or Aunt Carol he'll run away. Just give us a chance.'

'He isn't getting himself into more trouble, is he?' asked Aunt Carol anxiously.

Cheryl glanced at her mother, unsure what to say.

'Listen,' Mum said. 'I'm not very happy about this, but if it means getting Kev back, I think we should let them try.'

Aunt Carol nodded.

'OK, Cheryl,' said Mum. 'You've got half an hour. After that, we come looking for you.'

'So where *are* we going?' asked Helen.

'Andy Ramage's bonfire.'

'And you think he's there?'

'I'm not sure,' Cheryl admitted. 'But I know our Kev. He's taken about all he can stand. He's out for revenge.'

'Are you sure we shouldn't have brought your mum and Kev's along with us?'

'I'm not sure of anything. I'm not exactly his favourite person, either.'

'Then what …?'

Just then logic was the last thing Cheryl wanted to hear. 'Oh, give it a rest, Helen. One of these days you'll wear out that gob of yours.'

For once, Helen lapsed into shocked silence.

In ten minutes they were at the waste-ground.

'There's nobody here,' said Helen.

'It's early yet.'

Bangers were echoing in the distance, and while they waited they could make out the glow of far-off bonfires.

—— 135 ——

After a few minutes, Cheryl glanced at her watch. 'Maybe I was wrong.'

'I don't think so,' said Helen.

Andy Ramage was arriving with his usual crew.

'Here's Andy,' Cheryl murmured. 'But where's Kev?'

The moment they spotted the two girls watching them from a distance, the gang started hooting and jeering.

'You came after all, then?' Andy taunted. 'What's up, not got one of your own?'

'We're going to a display,' Helen countered.

'Ooh, a dis-plaay!' Andy whooped in derision. He flicked his nose. 'Aren't we posh?'

'Hey, Andy,' Tez shouted. 'Let's get this bommy lit.'

'No, wait,' said Cheryl anxiously.

'What's the matter with you?'

'I don't know.'

Andy sneered at her. 'You're crazy.' With that, he pulled a box of matches from his jacket pocket.

'Please, Andy,' Cheryl begged. 'Don't.'

Though the fire hadn't even been lit, the stench of burning was everywhere. The boys paused for a moment, then advanced on the bonfire.

'Did you hear something?' asked Helen.

'Like what?'

'I don't know. It's just that … Ow!'

'Now what?'

'Something hit me on the leg.'

They looked down to see a stone lying on the ground next to her shoe. Cheryl turned. That's when she saw him.

'Kevin!'

He was hiding behind a pile of rubble. Rooster was with him.

'Sh!' Kevin hissed. 'You'll spoil it.'

'What have you done?'

'Get over here with us, will you?'

'But why?'

'What do you think?' Kevin replied. 'We've fixed their bommy. Everything was going great till you turned up. We've been waiting for you to clear off.'

Cheryl had half-guessed what he was up to, but she hadn't wanted to believe it. 'How have you fixed it?'

Rooster chuckled. 'I found this council hut round our way. We nicked a load of fireworks. Not your shop-bought rubbish. This is the heavy-duty stuff for the big displays. Real big ones.'

'And you've planted them in the bonfire?'

'Got it in one,' said Kevin. 'We hid them earlier. I just want to see Brain Damage's face when they go up.'

Cheryl turned towards the bonfire. The drizzle earlier in the evening had made it difficult to light.

'Don't you understand?' she cried. 'If they're used in displays, they must be really powerful. Somebody could get hurt. Worse.'

Kevin's expression didn't change.

'Don't you care at all?' she asked.

His face remained dead-pan.

'Come on,' she demanded. 'What did you put in there?'

'Four boxes.'

'Four boxes! You mean those things in the bin-bags?'

Kevin nodded.

'Look,' said Helen.

Andy had succeeded in lighting a small fire at the base of the wooden pyramid.

'Think about it, Kev. That lot will go up like a bomb.'

Kevin turned slowly in the direction of the bonfire.

'Take no notice,' said Rooster. 'You wanted to get your own back, didn't you? This is what we talked about, Kev, the big one.'

'Kevin, somebody could get killed.' Cheryl was shaking. For the first time in her life, she was paralysed by fear. Madness was all around, clawing at her. 'Kev, this won't just give him a fright. You can't control something like this.'

Kevin stood rooted to the spot for a few moments. 'Can't control it,' he murmured.

'For goodness' sake, Kev,' said Cheryl.

He stared at her. No, *through* her.

'Dad,' he said. 'The fire. It was Dad. It was always him.'

'What are you talking about?' demanded Rooster impatiently.

'Everything that happened. All that I've been through …'

'Are you going to do this, or what?' asked Rooster.

'Leave him alone, you!' said Cheryl.

'All that wasted time,' said Kevin in a faltering voice. Then, as if awakening from a heavy sleep, he shook himself. 'Control it, I've got to control it.'

White smoke was beginning to belch from the drizzle-damp wood of the bonfire.

'What have I done?' he breathed as it began to spit and hiss. 'What the hell have I done?' He lunged forward and began stumbling towards the bonfire.

'Run!' he yelled. 'Get away from there.'

Andy and his gang didn't move. At first they just gaped in surprise, then surprise turned to fury.

'It's McGovern. Get him!'

Andy struck Kevin first, then Tez and the others joined in. Kevin didn't even try to defend himself against the flurry of kicks and punches.

'You don't understand,' he cried. 'Forget the feud. It's going to blow.'

By then, none of Andy's gang were interested in

—— 138 ——

listening. They had their enemy cornered and they weren't about to let him go.

'Stop it!' Cheryl screamed. 'He's telling the truth.'

The flames were climbing the bonfire, licking into the cracks between the outer timbers.

'Helen, Rooster,' she cried. 'You've got to help.'

'Count me out,' said Rooster. 'You've messed it up. I'm not hanging round to get caught.'

'Rooster!'

'Forget him,' barked Helen. 'Kev needs us.'

They began to run forward, waving and shouting. They had hardly covered half the distance when the bonfire exploded in a furious eruption of light and sound. The fire beast was spitting and belching in every direction.

'Down!' yelled Cheryl.

As she hit the floor, she could see Andy's gang fleeing in terror.

'But where's Kev?' asked Helen.

'Oh no.'

Barely two metres from the inferno lay Kevin. He wasn't moving.

Twenty-Eight

'*I*S HE ALL RIGHT?'

It was Aunt Pat. She'd burst through the doors of Casualty and grabbed the first nurse she saw.

Cheryl sank down in the hospital chair, trying to wish herself away. Helen had gone to phone her mum, so she was going to have to face the music alone.

'There's our Cheryl,' said Mum.

'Is Kevin all right?' Aunt Pat asked. 'That nurse didn't seem to know anything.'

'I don't know,' said Cheryl. 'We've just been waiting. Helen's here too.'

'What happened?' asked Mum. 'The hospital didn't really tell us anything over the phone.'

'There was this bonfire,' Cheryl began.

'A fire,' Aunt Carol interrupted. 'I might have guessed.'

Cheryl shrank back at the angry outburst.

'Don't worry, love. Carol's not shouting at you.'

'No,' said Aunt Carol. 'I'm worried, that's all. Look, I'm going to see if that nurse has found anything out for me yet. Pat, watch our Gareth for a minute.'

'But when are we going to the fireworks?' asked Gareth.

'We don't know yet,' said Mum. 'Here, do your colouring over there. I want to talk to Cheryl.'

Amazingly, Gareth did as he was told and knelt down by the drinks machine to colour.

'Now,' said Mum, sitting down on the seat next to Cheryl and taking her hand. 'Tell me what happened.'

'I'm scared, Mum.'

'I know, I know. Did Kevin get burned?'

'No,' said Cheryl. 'I don't think so. There was a big flash. It sort of knocked him over, then he wouldn't get up.'

'He was unconscious?'

Cheryl shook her head slowly. 'Not really. He was groaning. He said a few things.'

'And there were no burns? You're sure?'

Cheryl nodded.

'Thank God for that. But what was he up to?' Mum checked that Pat wasn't around. 'Was he playing with fire?'

'No!'

'The truth, Cheryl.'

Cheryl took a deep breath. I won't let you down, Kev, not this time. 'No.'

She realised Helen had returned from the phone. She was standing just behind Mum.

'He wasn't, was he, Helen?'

'No, Mrs Tasker.'

Cheryl could tell that her mother didn't believe them.

Helen slipped away to help Gareth with his colouring book.

'But what *was* he doing there?'

'He loves watching the fires. You know that. He was wrong to run away from Aunt Pat, but that's all he did.'

Her mother was watching her closely. It would need a better story than that.

'Kids,' said Mrs Tasker. 'Well, I don't know what to make of any of this.'

—— 141 ——

'Here's Aunty Carol,' said Cheryl.

'Well?' asked Mum. 'Do you know anything?'

'I've just seen him,' said Aunt Carol. 'They're letting him out in a few minutes. We've got to watch for delayed shock, but he seems all right. Oh, thank God he's OK. The doctor said you two were really good. By pulling him back from the fire like that you stopped him getting terrible burns. Do you know what, Pat, once they'd dragged him clear they hailed a passing motorist. Some young chap on his way home from work. He's the one who brought them to casualty. I just wish he'd stayed so I could have thanked him.'

'Well, it looks like there's no harm done,' said Mum.

'But what was Kev up to?' asked Aunt Carol. 'I can't get much sense out of him.'

'I think,' said Mum, 'we can talk about that later. He's not hurt, that's the main thing.'

'Yes,' said Aunt Carol. 'That's best. Oh, Cheryl …'

'Yes, Aunty Carol.'

'Kev's getting dressed. He was asking for you.'

Cheryl nodded and made her way to the curtained cubicle. 'Kev?'

Kevin had his back to her. He was perched on the bed, pulling his T-shirt over his head.

'I didn't give you away,' she said. 'I think I'll say you were having a row with Brain Damage. You were trying to spoil his bonfire. It's close enough to the truth, without mentioning the boxes of fireworks. It might just work. What do you think?'

That's when she realised. Kevin was crying. It was a long, wheezing, plaintive sound that made her want to reach out and comfort him.

'What's up? Is it hurting?'

A shake of the head.

'Is it because Rooster ran out on you?'

'No.' The word came out soft and strange.

'Then what?'

Kevin turned his head. His eyes were red.

'I remembered.'

'Remembered. Remembered what?'

'My dad.'

'What *are* you on about?'

'It's him. He made me like I am.'

'When he went away, you mean?'

Kevin hung his head. 'No, not that. You don't understand at all. I must have blocked it out, or something.'

Kev, you're talking in riddles.'

'He was like me. He wanted to be strong. He thought he could control the fire. You can't though, can you? It's stronger than anything. Maybe I was trying to live up to him doing this, too. It's always been there, in the back of my mind. Crazy, isn't it? I was the ghost that haunted Brain Damage. Dad's the ghost that haunts me.'

'Kev, you'll have to slow down. I don't get any of this.'

He stabbed at his forehead. 'It's in here. The whole thing. I must have only been little. They'd had a row, him and Mum. They used to have lots of them, though I never knew what they were about. This one evening it was really bad. Mum was yelling, asking him what sort of father he was. Then he was shouting back. I don't know what it was about, but I started crying, so mum says: Now look what you've done. That seemed to drive him mad. He snatched me up and dragged me out of the house.'

Cheryl felt uneasy. 'You don't need to tell me this, Kev.'

'I want to.' He paused, then corrected himself. 'I *need* to.'

'OK, I'm listening.'

—— 143 ——

'My dad was really angry,' Kevin continued. 'That's one of the things that sticks in my mind. There was a hardness about him. He was rough with me, shoving me into the car as if he didn't care about me one bit. Mum was banging on the car door, begging him to give me back. But he pulled away dead fast. I looked back and saw her running after the car. Then all the neighbours were in the street, wondering what was going on. We drove round for hours. I don't think Dad really knew what to do with me. It was obvious I was in the way. He took me out of temper, that's all. Anyway, we drove down near the docks, one of those little industrial estates. I looked out of the window, watching the street lights flashing past. I didn't know what was happening, but I was with my dad so I started to feel safe despite the way he was acting. I even stopped wondering why Mum had been crying.'

Kevin paused to wipe his eyes again.

'Safe? That's a laugh, isn't it? I still don't know what he was doing exactly. It must have been illegal, I know that much. An insurance job, or something.'

Cheryl barely understood what Kevin was talking about. That much must have been obvious from the expression on her face, because he began to explain himself.

'You know, when they torch a place to get the money on it. You know what I mean.'

There was an uneasy silence. When he finally resumed his story, he no longer seemed to care whether she understood or not.

'Anyway, Dad pulled up in front of this warehouse and got out of the car. He must have told me five or six times to stay in the car. No matter what, I had to stay put. So there I was in the back of the car, watching him walk away.'

Cheryl imagined the scene. The little boy in the car, alone with his fear. His father silent and ill-tempered, preoccupied with the task in hand.

'I can remember hearing this weird sound. Dong, dong, dong. Like somebody jumping up and down on a tin lid. After that it was silence. I didn't think he was coming back. I thought he was leaving me there. So you know what I did? I unfastened my seatbelt and went to look for him. There I was on this darkened street, scared out of my wits, wanting my dad. Then he was walking back towards me. I was just going to call to him when I saw him light this rag. It must have been soaked in petrol. That's when I realised what the funny sound was. In the other hand he had a metal can filled with the stuff. He just tossed the rag into the doorway of the warehouse and it went up like ... well, like that bonfire just now.'

'Oh, Kev.'

'He froze when he saw me. Mad, isn't it? There's this huge fire behind him and he's just standing there open-mouthed, like a kid caught with his hand in the sweetie jar. You know what? I think he was ashamed. Maybe he thought he wouldn't be my hero any more. How stupid can you get? It didn't make any difference. None at all. Because he was doing it, I thought it must be right. On the way back in the car he made me promise I'd never tell. I never did, either. I was so good at keeping the secret, I suppose I eventually managed to hide it from myself. Bits of it would come back to me at night when I was lying awake but I did my best to shut it out. It didn't end there, though. He'd sort of changed me. I was a thing of fire. It didn't matter too much till he left. I had other things, the good things, playing footy in the park, sparring with him in the yard, going out on trips. I was a thing of fire, but I was more than that. I had so much else. I had a life. Then when he went away, he killed all the good things. The fire was all I had left. It became everything.'

Cheryl didn't know what to say. She glanced nervously at the curtain.

'Your mum will come for us in a sec,' she said.

'I know.'

'So how do you feel about him now?'

'What am I supposed to feel? He's my dad. I know what he did was wrong, but I still want him back.'

'And your mum?'

'She'll never have him back. In a way, I think it was over between them the moment he took me like that. They stuck together for a few years, but he was always walking out and staying away for a few days. She just didn't trust him any more. One day he walked out and never came back.'

His story over, Kevin stood up abruptly. 'Dads, eh?' he said with a brightness that didn't ring true.

Chelyl smiled ruefully. Her own problems hadn't gone away but they suddenly didn't seem that bad. 'Yes, dads.'

And that's when Kevin sank helplessly against her. This time the tears came in long, cold streams touching her own face. Instinctively, she held him.

Cheryl heard the metal curtain-runners. It was her mum and Aunt Carol.

'Now this,' said Mum in a brave attempt at humour, 'This I don't believe.'

Twenty-Nine

'Y OU KNOW THE OTHER NIGHT,' SAID KEVIN.
    'Yes?'
'When did Helen go? I don't remember her leaving.'
'Her dad came to the hospital.'
'Oh, I didn't notice.'
'I know.'
There was a moment's silence, as they sat facing one another in Cheryl's room. It was their first chance to talk about the fire. Kevin had been shut away in his house for two days. The light was failing but it didn't bother them. They sat in the gathering gloom, full of thoughts of Bonfire night.
'Did I look stupid, blubbing like that?'
'No, everybody understood.'
'I hope not,' said Kev. 'Not everything.'
'Did your mum give you a hard time, after you got back from the hospital?'
'No, I was amazed. After Gareth went to bed, she just sat there rocking me in her arms. I started to feel a bit daft.'
'What about the next day when she'd had time to think about it?'
Kevin shook his head. 'She had a bit of a go, but she's been quiet really. I don't know what to make of it.'
'What did you tell her?' Cheryl asked. 'We'll have to get our stories right. I don't want to drop you in it.'

'More or less what you said that night. I said I was trying to knock Brain Damage's bonfire down, but he came and surprised me. I said I came back later and we had a fight. I think she believed that ... just about.'

'Really?'

'Oh, she knows there's a lot more to it, she told me that much. The funny thing is, she isn't going crazy on me like she used to. I think she knows I've changed.'

'Mum hasn't hassled me much either. Weird, isn't it?'

Kevin smiled. 'Don't complain. If they're going to forget it, why should I argue?'

Cheryl became serious. 'I wouldn't go that far. I don't think they've exactly *forgotten* it.'

'No, you're right. There was one thing Mum was really worried about.'

'What's that?'

'Willy finding out. Mum said I could get put into care or something.'

'Oh, they wouldn't!'

'I don't think so,' said Kevin. 'Mum makes things up to put the frighteners on me. Usually, I don't take any notice. But it scared me when she said it.'

There was a long silence, as each of them tried to work out how they felt. But words failed them. In the end they just sat, sharing one another's company, sharing the secret.

'I think it's over,' said Kevin finally.

'It better had be,' said Cheryl.

'No, I don't mean that. The fire. I think it's out of my system. Mum feels it too. I just wish I understood how.'

'Is it worth worrying about? I reckon we're better just getting on with our lives.'

'Yeah, I suppose so. I just hope Brain Damage lets me.'

'He's been quiet at school,' said Cheryl, with a half-smile.

'Has he? I must have scared him witless. He must think I'm a real psycho. Touch wood, that'll keep him quiet.'

'Don't let it bother you. He doesn't matter. Just remember. When Brain Damage tries to get on your back, we'll be there.'

Kev looked away, as if embarrassed. 'That's what Bashir said, too.'

'See, so you aren't on your own.'

Kevin sighed. 'It won't stop us getting our heads kicked in.'

'You never know. We'll win people round again. Besides, at least we'll get our heads kicked in together.'

Kev gave a wry smile. 'Now there's a comforting thought.'

After that, there was no more to say. Not another word was spoken until Aunt Carol called up the stairs.

'Time to go, Kev.'

'Can't we stay a bit longer?' asked Kevin.

'Not tonight. It's a bit late for Gareth.'

'OK, coming.'

Cheryl followed Kevin downstairs and hung around in the hallway with him while Mum found something else to talk to Aunt Carol about.

'Mu-um,' groaned Gareth.

'OK, love,' said Aunt Carol. 'You've been very patient. I've just got to give these to Pat.'

'Your ciggies!'

'Yes, it's about time I had another go at giving up. And you're going to help.'

'Me. How?'

'By keeping out of trouble.'

Kevin nodded and opened the front door.

'Hang on,' said Cheryl, her heart turning over. 'Who's this?'

Somebody was sitting on the step. It was an adult, but the hunched, lonely figure appeared almost childlike.

'Dad,' said Cheryl. 'Does this mean …?'

'Your visit made me think,' he said, getting up. 'You were right. It *is* simple. So here I am. I had my grand entrance planned. I'd memorized this little speech too, but when I got here I was too scared to ring the bell. I suppose I'm not the really the hero type. Pat,' he continued hesitantly. 'Do you think I could come in? I mean …'

Cheryl's mum nodded. The expression on her face gave nothing away. 'I know what you mean.'

'So can I?'

Cheryl's mother turned and started rummaging amongst the pile of bills and circulars by the phone.

'What's she after?' hissed Kevin.

'Beats me,' said Cheryl. What was wrong with a big hug and welcome home? Don't say Mum was turning funny too?

'Pat?'

Cheryl's dad was getting as fidgety as she was.

'Remember this, Dave Tasker?' said her mother, brandishing the college prospectus. 'You come back. I go to college. Deal?'

'Deal,' Dad agreed. With a nervous cough, he squeezed into the crowded hallway. 'What is this, anyway?' he asked. 'Family convention? Has something happened while I've been away?'

That did it. Suddenly everybody was laughing. Laughing till the tears came.

'It wasn't that funny, was it?' he asked.

'Yes,' said Mum, squeezing his arm. 'It was actually.'

'Anyway,' said Aunt Carol. 'This time we are off. I'll

ring you tomorrow, Pat. Oh, and Dave, good to see you back.'

Leaving her mother and father to talk, Cheryl remained at the front door-step and watched Aunt Carol, Gareth and Kevin until they were out of sight. She raised her face to meet the freshening wind off the Mersey. The smell of bonfires seemed to hang faintly in the air. The funny thing was, this time it didn't bother her at all.

also by Alan Gibbons

Chicken

'All I could think about was Webbo and what he had in store for me.'

Davy's too chicken to stand up to bullying at school. He's been singled out as an easy target. His family aren't much help – they're all chicken too. Mum's frightened of learning to drive, big brother Col is terrifying himself trying to impress his new friends. And Dad has too many problems of his own to be sympathetic.

But in the end it's his little sister's strange secret which spurs Davy on . . . and surprises the whole family as well.

Ganging Up

John and Gerry have always been friends, brought together by their passion for football. Then Gerry's dad loses his job and everything turns sour. The two boys had always steered clear of the gangs at school, but Gerry gets drawn in and now he and John find themselves standing on opposite sides.

Set in a tough inner city Liverpool estate, this is a story about friendships, rivalries and survival played out at school and on the football field.

The Edge

Danny is a boy on the edge. A boy teetering on the brink of no return, living in fear.

Cathy is his mother. She's been broken by fear.

Chris Kane is fear – and they belong to him.

But one day they escape. They're looking for freedom, for the promised land where they can start really living. Instead they find prejudice, and danger of another kind.

Uncompromising and disturbing, but utterly readable, Alan Gibbons' latest novel positively crackles with tension as he writes about a mother and her son desperate to start a new life.

Whose Side Are You On

Some things are worth fighting for . . .

Mattie likes a quiet life. When the school bullies start picking on his Asian friend, Pravin, he knows he should do something about it. Too scared to act, Mattie runs away. But instead of escaping, somehow he is transported to the very heart of slavery, a sugar plantation in eighteenth-century Jamaica, not knowing whether he will return home . . .

Shadow of the Minotaur

'Real life' or the death defying adventures of the Greek myths, with their heroes and monsters, daring deeds and narrow escapes – which would you choose?

For Phoenix it's easy. He hates his new home and the new school where he is bullied. He's embarrassed by his computer geek dad. But when he logs on to the Legendeer, the game his dad is working on, he can be a hero. He is Theseus fighting the terrifying Minotaur, or Perseus battling with snake-haired Medusa.

The trouble is The Legendeer is more than just a game. Play it if you dare.

Vampyr Legion

What if there are real worlds where our nightmares live and wait for us?

Phoenix has found one and it's alive. Armies of blood-sucking vampyrs and terrifying werewolves, the creatures of our darkest dreams, are poised to invade our world.

But Phoenix has encountered the creator of *Vampyr Legion*, the evil Gamesmaster, before and knows that this deadly computer game is for real – he must win or never come back.

Caught in the Crossfire

'You know what happens to people like you? You get hit in the crossfire.'

Shockwaves sweep the world in the aftermath of 11 September. The Patriotic League barely need an excuse in their fight to get Britain back for the British, but this is chillingly perfect.

Rabia and Tahir are British Muslims, Daz and Jason are out looking for trouble, Mike and Liam are brothers on different sides. None of them will escape unscarred from the terrifying and tragic events which will weave their lives together.

Marking a new dimension in his writing on race, riots and real life *Caught in the Crossfire* is an unforgettable novel that Alan Gibbons needed to write.

'Gibbons' writing often addresses worrying issues of social justice but never as powerfully as in this novel . . . the writing – the short, sharp pieces that take us into the mind of each character – is accessible and compulsive.'
Wendy Cooling, *The Bookseller*